CW00553287

EVEN THE GODS FEAR IT

EVEN THE GODS FEAR IT

KB

Kelly Barker

Copyright © 2023 Kelly Barker

The moral right of the author has been asserted.

Apart from any fair dealing for the purposes of research or private study,
or criticism or review, as permitted under the Copyright, Designs and Patents
Act 1988, this publication may only be reproduced, stored or transmitted, in
any form or by any means, with the prior permission in writing of the
publishers, or in the case of reprographic reproduction in accordance with
the terms of licences issued by the Copyright Licensing Agency. Enquiries
concerning reproduction outside those terms should be sent to the publishers.

This is a work of fiction. Names, characters, businesses, places, events
and incidents are either the products of the author's imagination
or used in a fictitious manner. Any resemblance to actual persons,
living or dead, or actual events is purely coincidental.

Matador
Unit E2 Airfield Business Park,
Harrison Road, Market Harborough,
Leicestershire. LE16 7UL
Tel: 0116 2792299
Email: books@troubador.co.uk
Web: www.troubador.co.uk/matador
Twitter: @matadorbooks

ISBN 978 1803136 127

British Library Cataloguing in Publication Data.
A catalogue record for this book is available from the British Library.

Printed and bound in the UK by TJ Books LTD, Padstow, Cornwall
Typeset in 11pt Adobe Garamond Pro by Troubador Publishing Ltd, Leicester, UK

Matador is an imprint of Troubador Publishing Ltd

Dedicated to Rory and Penny

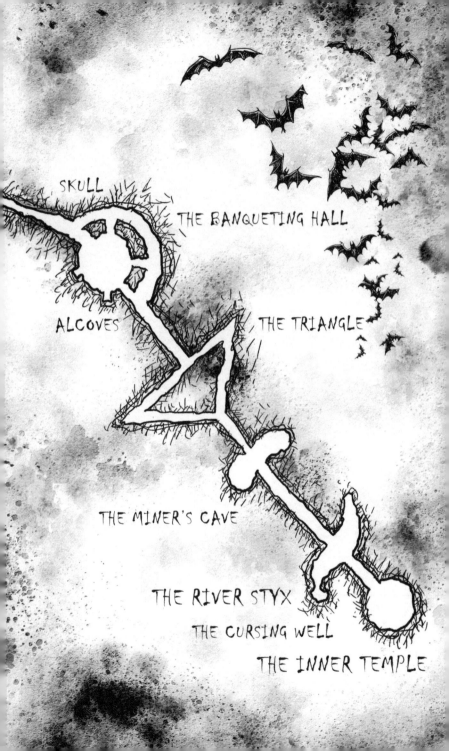

CHAPTER 1

David was right: the bookshop was starting to look empty. It had been almost a year since he had died – or more accurately, was killed, I should say. One of my characters from the story I was writing snapped his neck while I was on the phone to him. A vampire called Ivy wanted revenge because I had deleted her story while she was no longer within it. I erased her home and her family. In her reality, I killed her father, and then she killed mine. But I couldn't lose David; he was all the family I had, so I wrote a story about him and brought him back to life. Sort of anyway. The only way I really knew how to do it was to recreate him as a phantom, a ghost, just like our dog, Goodboy. He had become my version of a ghost, I suppose; it wasn't like I had ever seen one. Some people would say they don't exist; well, they do now. The fact was that I had very few choices regarding his resurrection. I couldn't exactly bring him back as the human he'd once been; the coroner had pronounced his death an accident at the scene.

"Zoe, will you cut my hair?" Varik asked for the third time, while pulling his black fringe over his nose. He was wearing his usual black jeans and slim-fit black jumper.

I looked down at what I was wearing; my usual too. "No. I don't cut hair any more," I snapped. We had more important things to discuss. David, Bowen, Varik and I were in David's – now mine – second-hand bookshop, discussing a new plan of action to save the plesiosaurs. Another creation of mine, and another disaster. Although, in my defence, I wasn't fully aware that I could write characters and bring them into existence back then.

"You still cut Bowen's hair, you little liar," he whined.

Yeah, whined. A whining vampire, and another creation of mine. As I said, they have all been disasters so far. Well, apart from Goodboy. As if sensing my thoughts, he bounded over to me for a bit of attention. His once emaciated form had transformed to one of pure muscle and strength.

"Yeah, I do." I blushed, then I looked away. "But it's different."

"How so?" he asked.

At the same time, Bowen looked over and winked at me.

But Varik misses nothing. "Ah, it's like that, is it? A role-play thing, is it?"

"No," I snapped at Varik again.

I saw David smile awkwardly, then look the other way – at nothing in particular. I hid my face in my hands, knowing Varik would not take the hint and keep his mouth shut.

Bowen laughed without embarrassment and asked, "Varik, what do you know about role-play?"

"A lot, thanks to you and that online fishing page you set up for me." Varik shivered.

We all bloody shivered when he brought *that* up.

He needed blood to survive. You could argue that's how

he was created, and he therefore shouldn't be judged by it. I certainly didn't judge him. However, he couldn't go round feeding from and killing humans – not the innocent ones anyway. Bowen had set him up with an online profile as a twelve-year-old little girl, which was based on something he learned from his time in the police force. Within an hour, he had six men asking if he – or she, I should say – was home alone. One of them even sent a dick pic and asked for a 'front bottom' pic in return. I retched when he first told me that. Varik would then arrange to meet with these paedophiles. Some may say murder is murder, but I say the world was now a better place.

Varik had that gleam in his eyes, and I knew he wasn't finished. I was about to ask Bowen if he wanted a coffee, but Varik put his hand over my mouth, cutting me off. "Bowen goes to the barber shop to get his hair cut by this lusty she-barber. But, oh no, he has no money. How will he pay?" He grinned widely, revealing his serrated, pointed teeth.

"No, absolutely not," I said, but my words were muffled behind his hand. I pushed his arm out of the way. How did he know? I looked at Bowen. "Did you tell him?"

"No, I didn't," Bowen said, failing to hide his smirk behind the back of his hand.

"*Right, that's it,*" I shouted, then I headed towards the staffroom.

Bowen and Varik just laughed it off, which both pissed me off and filled me with joy. My temper deflated instantly. I was happy for them both, if I were honest. They got on so well, and I couldn't have asked for more than that.

I flipped the kettle on, then walked back into the shop. "Look, we need to discuss what we're going to do next to help my plesiosaurs."

They were being hunted ruthlessly, and we were running

out of time. Nations from around the globe couldn't forge an agreement on how best to protect them, which resulted in the poaching of my beautiful, docile creatures becoming a free-for-all. Three of them were already in tanks, and although it had been disguised under the name of 'scientific research', those tanks were in amusement parks. And the parks' admission price had risen to something that only those with more money than sense would pay.

It should be the right of all sentient creatures to sleep in peace, and to live a life with dignity and free from torment. Every time a plesiosaur was killed or caught, an unrecognisable emotion burned through me. It was a pure, seething, black hatred, the likes of which I had never experienced. I wanted those poachers to die.

"We're going around in circles, poppet. All we can do is to continue supporting the anti-poaching fleets," David said.

That was easier said than done. Many of the so-called 'environmental' and 'research' vessels now concealed their harpoons. It was difficult determining friend from foe.

"You could create bigger ships, with more of my kind on board," Varik suggested again, for the tenth time. "You are the Watcher; you have the power."

The Watcher. He was right: I am. The name was given to me by my own character. I looked over at Bowen, and he shook his head to say no. He wasn't as at ease with my 'abilities' as I first thought. He often questioned David about his current state, asking him how he felt about not needing food, where he went when he wasn't with us, how he felt when he died and about being brought back. He told me about how Harry, the *AmberIvy*'s captain, couldn't remember his past. Harry had asked Bowen if he had any family; this broke my heart. No, Harry didn't have a family because I hadn't given him one when I wrote about him. I could no longer create beings without consequences, and yet I had a yearning to explore my abilities and to know my limitations.

"Another ship then," I offered pointlessly.

I had created the *AmberIvy* for Bowen to help the other anti-poaching fleets. He and Varik had returned after having spent just over three long months aboard it. I had missed him every day, and thought about him every minute of that day, but at the same time, I was grateful he was out there, sabotaging those hunters.

"No, sweetheart." He smiled, then moved to stand next to me. "I can't believe I'm going to say this, but perhaps we should let them go. They don't belong here in this time period anyway."

"You don't mean that." I frowned, confused by his change of heart.

"I do." He looked defeated, almost ashamed.

"I thought you were going back up there. Are you staying now?" I was both disappointed with him and relieved. My warring emotions really pissed me off when they couldn't make up their minds.

"No, I'm going. It will be my last three months, though. I believe we've already lost, but that doesn't mean I want to make it easy for the poachers." He leaned against David's desk and opened his arms for me to walk into them.

"Varik, are you going back on the *AmberIvy*?" I asked.

"No, I'm staying to keep you company." He smirked at Bowen. "The ocean isn't my thing, and thanks to you, I still have a lot to learn about this world."

Ah, yes he did. I had written a story about a kingdom of vampires being trapped in the Inner Temple, a place that exists within the Hellfire Caves in West Wycombe. I had written that they had been trapped for twenty-eight years, and they were starving because they could no longer access the human realm. A human realm they had never truly seen or been to because I began the story while they were trapped, yet I needed to create a yearning and a desire in them to want to be free. Again, I did this not knowing about my abilities at the time. When Goodboy was cruelly taken from this world, I wanted to give him a new one – one filled with love. I had added him to the story and gave him to Varik. When I deleted Ivy's story and her home as she knew it, I spared both Varik and Goodboy, with the thought of writing a new path for them.

Bowen looked uneasy; perhaps he wasn't happy about the two of us spending time together. It wasn't jealousy. He knew how much he meant to me: I had happily agreed to become his wife one day. I looked down at my beautiful ring; he had chosen a black sapphire. He had told me it was because I was different. Varik had said it was because he was cheap. I smiled at the memory, then I realised why Bowen would be unhappy about him staying behind with me. Varik could behave like a child in a toy shop when the parent said no, and in comparison to the Inner Temple – his previous home – the human world was indeed a toy shop.

"Three more months, Varik; come on," Bowen pleaded. "We don't leave for another two weeks."

"No. Anyway, the sun is down, and I have a date with a fifty-two-year-old man who has requested I wear my hair in pigtails, and at this rate" – he looked at me with a fake sad smile, then pulled at his fringe again – "I will be able to put my hair into pigtails."

"Fine, I'll cut it for you," I sighed.

***

Bowen was leaving in four days, and until then, he would work with me at the shop. His plan was to take a couple of years off from the police force to fight for my plesiosaurs, then rejoin. It turned out he wasn't the only police officer to do this. His ex-colleague Officer Blake had also done the same and was now a crew member on a ship called the *Ocean Warriors*. But I really enjoyed working with Bowen, so hopefully, when he does rejoin, he'll spare a couple of hours here and there to work in the shop with me. Bowen had also helped me set up an online bookshop that had proved very successful – although David would say otherwise. His shop used to be stacked to the point that the books had no shelf space. Even though you could now see the floor, the shop had somehow lost its identity.

"Sweetheart, I'm going to take these to the post office. What did you want for lunch?" Bowen asked.

"Same as usual, please. Bowen, are you okay? You've been quiet today." He hadn't been sleeping well either, and I would know. Resisting sleep was a God-given talent I was born with. The realm I often lived in, somewhere between being asleep and awake, was my true domain.

He put the bag down and cupped the back of my head with his hand. "You don't know? I'm going to miss you. The three months I was away from you was hard on me."

"I know. It was hard for me too. You don't have to go, but if you do, as you said, it will be the last time." I caressed his face and kissed him before he could answer. "You have a few days to think about it."

I also knew how dangerous it had been out there. Varik had told me an illegal poachers' ship collided with theirs one night, and a few of the poachers crew boarded the *AmberIvy*. They obviously thought the *AmberIvy* was full of hippies and tree-huggers who would scare easily. Varik tore them to pieces, then threw their bodies overboard. The crew from the illegal ship didn't even call it in; they couldn't.

"I already feel downhearted, and if I don't see this through, I'll feel worse for it. I want to feel that I did everything I possibly could, you know?" Bowen declared.

"I do know, and that's why I love you so much. Why don't I close the shop for two days, and we can make the most of the time we have?"

"Yeah, let's do that." He lifted my hand and kissed me just above my engagement ring. He sighed.

"There's something else; what is it?" My heart hammered.

I always felt on edge with Bowen, as if I could lose him at any moment. Being with me was a lot; I understood that – I really did. He always made sure I wasn't writing or made me talk it through with him first, which usually resulted in him saying, "No way, are you mad?" Yet he was fine with the *AmberIvy*, and he accepted the plesiosaurs, Captain Harry, Goodboy and the vampires. He was friends with one. But he couldn't accept David's current form. They'd grown close, and Bowen loved him, but he said it crossed a line. I used Goodboy as an example, but he said it was different. He said I didn't know better back then and there was a difference between a dog and human.

"Varik told you what happened on the ship," he sighed again. "Zoe, if something were to happen … if I died—"

"Bowen, why would you say that?" *Where did that come from?* I thought.

His face was unreadable. "If I died, I wouldn't want you to bring me back. Okay?"

"Why? Why wouldn't you want to come back to me?" I felt hurt. If it were me, I would not want to be separated from him. I took a hold of his arms and pulled him close to me.

"I would always want to come back to you, but I believe that once you're gone, you're gone. David's back, and he's not just some figment of your imagination; he is back as himself – as in his memories, personality … Oh, I don't know."

"But that's good; it's the real him." I furrowed my brow.

"Okay, how about this? You don't believe in heaven or the afterlife, correct? But I do. What if David is stuck here and can't go to heaven? What if I die and come back like him, and then you die?"

"What do you mean?" I stroked his hair away from his eyes.

"If both David and I are ghosts – your version of a ghost – and you die, er … in an accident or something, we would be stuck here. If there's a heaven, and I believe there is, I would want to be reunited there, not stuck here without you."

"Oh." I hadn't thought of that.

"Come here." He wrapped his arms around me. "Promise me, please, that you won't bring me back?"

Not an option. For the first time in my life, I had everything I had ever wanted. "Or I could write a story about how all my creations die when I die."

He clearly hadn't expected me to say that, and the surprise showed on his face. "No. Zoe, sweetheart, you don't even know the extent of your abilities. People like you don't even have a name. There are no myths or legends about what you can do."

It was true; we had done so much research over the last year, trying to find out about my abilities, why I had them and if there was someone else out there like me. Nothing came up. I remember being disappointed, and I still am. I couldn't just have this ability and not discover its full potential. I felt like a bloody sorceress. But at the same time,

I couldn't lose Bowen; he was more important to me. When we needed to kill Ivy after she killed David, I wrote myself into my own story and gave myself the ability to move and manipulate objects. Bowen asked me not to do it in front of him because it made him uneasy, so I didn't. However, when he was at sea, I practised. It turns out it was quite unpredictable anyway. I remember trying to pick up a coffee cup, but it fell to the floor. I was angry at myself and I tried again; it splintered. It was fair to say that my telekinesis was tethered to my emotions, or perhaps it was like a muscle: something that needed to be exercised.

"I know that, but what do I do, wait until I die to see you again? And what if you're wrong and there is no afterlife?" I sighed.

"What if there is?" He ran his hands down my back. "Let's not talk about this any more. We need to make the most of our time together, okay?" He stepped back, picked up the packages and walked out the door.

Was he right? I've just never been a believer in the afterlife or heaven, which is ironic if you think about it. Either way, I had to respect his wishes, and what's the point in even thinking about it? No one will be taking him away from me, and he will not die. Maybe I should convince Varik to go with him, just in case?

I called out to David to ask his opinion on the matter.

***

Waking up to Bowen stroking the hair from my face is something I will never take for granted. *Wait, something doesn't feel right.*

"Hmm, Bowen?" I slurred. My eyes were glued together with eye-bogies.

"Yes, it's me, your lover boy." Varik shrieked with laughter.

"*Oh, get the fuck out of my bed, you fucking creep!*" I shouted.

I couldn't jump out of bed because I was naked. Both our dogs, Missy and Goodboy, started jumping around and wagging their tails like complete loons. They obviously thought this was funny too. *What the hell?*

"How did you get in?" I demanded.

"You left your keys in the front door. Did you forget Bowen left?" He was still laughing, while lying across my bed.

"Please, have mercy on me, Varik. I feel like shit when he's not around, and I miss him already."

Bowen left three days ago, and I felt empty. Luckily, I had the shop to distract me and the dogs to keep me company, which kept my mind busy, but it wasn't the same. Varik, however, could take your mind off anything, but the stress that accompanied it was something I could do without.

"Poor little Watcher. Listen, Bowen put me in charge of you." He poked my nose with his clawed finger. "So, here I am."

"No, he didn't."

"He did. He told me to make sure you ate, slept and didn't get into trouble."

Oh, he did. Again, my emotions were at war. I was both furious and overwhelmed with Bowen's concern for me. I wondered if he knew I'd begged Varik to go with him and protect him aboard the *AmberIvy*. Obviously, Varik had refused.

"Well, as you can see, I've been sleeping, and if you go into the kitchen, you'll see three days' worth of dirty plates and cutlery in the sink," I suggested.

"And when was the last time you showered, Watcher? You smell vile, even to me." He smirked.

I blushed and giggled. *Yeah, I should probably have a shower.* My greasy hair was starting to stick to my scalp, and it was getting too knotty to brush. "The sun's up. You'll be trapped here all day while I'm at work."

"It's Sunday. What shall we do today, Watcher? I feel like getting into trouble, don't you?"

"You just said you're here to keep me out of trouble. Which is it?"

He answered with a grin.

He was after something; I could sense it.

"You can't leave the house unless I blindfold you and guide you everywhere. I'm not doing that today," I told him.

When I created my vampires, I wanted my own spin on them. I didn't want the sun to kill them, but I still felt that it should be one of their weaknesses. I gave them night vision and took away their ability to see in the sun.

"We don't need to leave the house for what we are going to get up to," he explained.

"Okay. What's the plan then?" I yawned into my fist.

"We" – he pulled my laptop from behind his back – "are going to write another story. You and me together. With my guidance, we will write something epic."

I hadn't written in ages, even though I had thought about it every day. That being said, I was still writing in my head. I could feel excitement pulsing through my veins, which was quickly followed by guilt. "Bowen wouldn't like it."

"Bowen's not here, is he?" He lifted both eyebrows.

"I can't. He'll be upset, and there's nothing I could write about that wouldn't impact the world." I did have a story in mind, though. I wanted to write about sleep demons: demons that ate your dreams for nourishment. Unfortunately, such a story could never be told – not by me anyway.

"That's where I come in." Varik interrupted my thoughts. "We'll revisit the Inner Temple and write a new story. You could create thousands of my kind, and I could be their leader – their king."

I couldn't help but laugh; I knew he was joking. Then I looked into those green eyes set into his perfectly sculpted face. All my creations had my eyes; something David and I couldn't work out. I sensed a sliver of sadness behind his cocky demeanour. What must it be like to be the only one of your kind? Was it lonely? Did he want a female to share his life with?

"You'd go back to the Inner Temple?" I queried. That place had become his prison.

"If I were king and could leave anytime I wished. I read this book about a man who could teleport around the world." He jumped off my bed and started pacing the length of my room. "He could only teleport to places he'd been to at first, but by the end of the book, all he had to do was look at a photo of the destination. You know, Watcher, we could both have that ability if you wanted it."

I knew which book he was talking about; I had read it too, many years ago. I smiled and imagined what it would be like to be able to teleport around the world. *I could visit Bowen. No, I couldn't do that; he'd give me a bollocking. I could teleport to work and back. No, I couldn't do that either; that was Missy's morning walk. Umm, what else?*

"I don't know, Varik; a lot could go wrong. I'd have to talk it through with David, and I already know what he'd say." David wasn't as strict as Bowen, but I knew he'd say no to teleportation. "What else?"

"What could possibly go wrong? Come on." He kicked my bed.

An adult tantrum was brewing, I could feel it, and if it didn't happen, then it would be him badgering me all day. I didn't know which was worse. "A lot can go wrong. We don't know enough about teleportation."

"But I do. Wait there." He left my room.

I was about to dress quickly when he re-entered.

"Everything we need to know is in this book." He held it up proudly.

I wrapped the duvet around my chest and leaned forwards to take it. "I'll have to reread it first." I knew in my heart I shouldn't be entertaining this, but curiosity always got the better of me.

"Why can't you just go with it? Watcher, you are a powerful being; why won't you embrace it?" He walked over to Bowen's wardrobe and took out a pair of shoes from the rack below.

"Put those back, Varik. Look, I want to embrace it; I do. But I have to be cautious. A woman died last year because of me, and Ivy … Well, you know."

He did know, and yet he never held it against me. He never blamed or resented me for his existence. He just accepted it. However, I still felt like I owed him in some way.

He put on Bowen's shoes, then frowned at me. "Why do you care so much for these humans? There are plenty of them."

"These days, I don't care so much – not after what they're doing to my plesiosaurs and not after the things you told me about those disgusting paedos." I shook my head to dislodge the thoughts. "But Amber was innocent, and I will never forgive myself."

I didn't really know for certain whether I was the cause of Amber's death, and yet I believed I was. Bowen believed Goodboy did it when he re-entered the human realm for the first time. He had been abused by his previous owners, and Bowen believed that Goodboy would have been disorientated and scared, and so he may have attacked out of fear. Amber was jogging at the time, and she sadly came to be known as 'the jogger' after her death. We think Goodboy perhaps thought she was chasing him; we'll never truly know.

"I understand why you like the innocent ones. How about this, then? There is only one of me, and more than I can count of humans that hurt innocent children. I say we need more of my kind."

There, he said it again. He pointed out that there is only one of him, and has asked for more of his kind. And I knew deep down he didn't really care about human life – whether it was a child's or not. But was it more of his kind he really wanted, or perhaps just one? I had often seen a yearning in his eyes every time Bowen wrapped his arms around me. My heart bled for him. I had two choices: I could grant Varik happiness or I could hurt Bowen. But Bowen would want Varik to be happy, wouldn't he? He was a part of our family now.

"Varik, I think I know what you really want. You'd have to police them, or her, yourself. You'd have to make them, or her, understand who is on the menu and who isn't."

He looked down, almost ashamed that I had guessed his thoughts. He grinned, then his expression changed again; this time, to one of sorrow. I couldn't keep up.

He quietly said, "I want my own female."

I should have taken the time to think this through. I probably should have talked this through with Bowen, but

Varik's admission made my mind up. How could I say no? Who was I to deny him?

"Okay, let me think this through. We'll start with a small number of survivors. I'll go back to the start of your story, when the Inner Temple was first overtaken by the demon armies. There are many gateways in the Hellfire Caves." I was talking more to myself than to Varik. "Let's say that, after the queen died, some vampires were able to escape in time to another realm, using a different gateway."

"Yes, Watcher. What else?"

"First, you need to take off Bowen's shoes, and then I'll need a coffee. I don't suppose you'd make me one?" I yawned.

"No, because I need a new pair." He shook his head slowly, then smirked. "And definitely not."

CHAPTER 2

The pair of us were in my living room, arguing over the Hellfire Caves map. There were many sections to the caves with really cool names. I wanted to use the Catacombs section for my new gateway, but Varik favoured the Cursing Well. I hadn't written a thing yet.

"It's too close to the River Styx, and I don't know enough about it." I yawned into my hand, feeling more drained than when I had first woken up.

Varik blinked at me. "Why does it matter?"

"Because it does. Look at the map. To enter the Inner Temple, you'll have to cross the River Styx. Why is the Cursing Well section tucked in between?"

"Maybe it was the only gateway accessible without needing obol coins for the Ferryman. Think about it. You wanted to keep the vampires from the human realm, right? What if the Cursing Well led to another realm?"

He was standing right over my shoulder while I was sitting at the table. I hadn't realised how important this was to him, and I wondered why he hadn't asked months ago. Oh, yeah, I did know: he waited until Bowen was out of the way. Was I allowing him to take advantage of the situation because I wanted to take advantage of it too? I was riddled with guilt, but why should I be?

"Okay, we'll go with the Cursing Well. Who's the gatekeeper and what is the payment?" My gatekeepers, such as the Ferryman, needed payment to cross the boundaries. The Ferryman took obols, and another of my gatekeepers, the Mistletoe Bride, wanted a sixpence. She was already the gatekeeper of the Banqueting Hall, which led to Minster Lovell – a ruin near my home town.

"Why does there have to be a gatekeeper?" he snapped.

"Because," I snapped back, "nothing in life is free, and I can't write a story where the trapped vampires just decided to walk out of a gateway. It needs to be realistic for it to work."

"Okay, what are you thinking?"

"Okay, let me google it and see what it comes up with." I typed in my query. "Here. The Cursing Well is filled with unholy water. It was used to baptise new members, er… before joining the satanic club prior to them crossing the River Styx to the Inner Temple."

I sighed, and Varik didn't look impressed.

"We'll go with the Catacombs," he said.

For fuck's sake! I leaned over my laptop, feeling even more drained. Varik really did suck the life out of you. *Can I put up with this for three more months or do I beg Bowen to come back?*

"The Catacombs are near the entrance. If they could get to the Catacombs, then why didn't they just walk out into the human realm?"

"I don't know; you wanted to use the Catacombs."

"I was talking to myself." I lifted my coffee cup; it was empty – again. It was always bloody empty. "Why were all the vampires in the Inner Temple at the time of the attack?"

"Watcher, only you know the answer to that question."

"I'm still talking to myself. Right, check this out. All vampires were called back at the time of the attack to defend the queen, not Ivy, her mother. Well, what if they didn't all make it back in time? What if a few went back, saw the carnage and retreated?"

"That would be treason. They would have been decapitated." He was not pleased by this; I had forgotten he'd fought in that war. He was the sole survivor.

"Who would decapitate them if there was no one left to do it?" I questioned.

He was probably thinking he would have, but he needed to understand that his kingdom had fallen. I could sit here and tell him it was all made up and none of it ever existed, but it did. I had the proof of its existence standing behind me, breathing down my neck.

"There has to be another way. I don't want to be the king of treacherous vampires."

"You will never be the king. They didn't exist in your world, remember? Only queens did. And if you're willing to bend the rules to suit you, then you can bend the rules to pardon the others." I looked over my shoulder to gauge his thoughts.

He shook his head. "No soldier would have abandoned their queen. Find another way." He put his hands on either side of my head, then forced it back to face my screen.

Wanting to get this right for him I racked my mind. Was he picking holes in my story because he didn't want his people back as desperately as I'd first thought? He had confirmed to me that he wanted a female, and maybe, for now, that was all he wanted. "Maybe she wasn't a soldier. Maybe she was very young when her parents hid her in the Catacombs, before they went to war."

He squeezed my shoulder, hard.

"Ow."

"Sorry. What's her name?"

"I don't know yet. I think she still lives in the Catacombs. I think she walks out into the human realm to feed, then she returns by morning." My heart fluttered with excitement. I really did miss making up stories.

"And?"

"And ... that's a good start, I think. Leave it with me."

***

It made very little difference whether you were a barber or bookseller: Monday mornings were gruelling – especially when you hadn't slept the night before. I had stayed up late and made a good start on Varik's story, and although his female still didn't have a name yet, her story was coming along smoothly. I fired up my laptop and started where I left off.

"Morning, poppet. What are you doing there?" David appeared from behind the shelves.

Coffee splashed all over the keyboard when I jumped. I shouldn't have felt guilty for writing, but I did. Heat crept over my face. "Hey, David. I'm working on something for Varik. Have you been with Bowen?" I said, while standing to hug him hello.

When David wasn't here, he was on the *AmberIvy*. It made me feel that little bit closer to Bowen, knowing that David had just been with him. It somehow seemed to close the distance.

"I was, and yes, he's fine. He'll be phoning you later today. What are you working on for Varik?" He looked concerned, but he needn't have, I knew what I was doing.

"A short story. Varik wants a female. Is Goodboy with Bowen? I haven't seen him all morning." Goodboy normally joined and enjoyed my morning walk with Missy.

"Yeah, he is. A female? Are you sure you should be doing that? Bowen didn't mention it."

"I only started it yesterday, and why do I need to tell Bowen everything?" I felt rotten for my snappy reply.

"He only worries, as do I. Will you be telling him?" David looked at me suspiciously.

"If I tell him, he'll tell me to stop. I'll wait until I'm done."

"Zoe, why are you being like that?" He looked surprised at what I had said.

"I don't know. I've really missed writing, and I didn't realise how much until yesterday." After I finally got rid of Varik, I was able to fly with it. It kept my mind off the heartache of missing Bowen, and made me feel somewhat unshackled.

"Just be honest with him. It's not like he can do much about it anyway," he sighed. "Let me read it, then."

We both smiled slyly at each other. Maybe he had missed it too.

"Before you do, help me think of a name for her. I have Lydia or Harper. To me, Lydia sounds as if she could be shy and perhaps a little unsure of herself. Harper, however, sounds like she could be a royal pain in the arse." I smirked, knowing which one he would pick.

"Let's go with Harper."

"Harper it is." I scrolled through from the start, and replaced the word 'female' with her new name.

"She won't be anything like Ivy will she?"

His innocent question stung. Ivy just wanted revenge for her father; something I would have done. She was more like me than any other character I had created. "No, Ivy was a queen. Harper is an orphan. Her parents hid her during the battle, which happened when she was only six. That would make her thirty-four now. Wait, Varik was trapped for twenty-eight years a year ago. She'd be thirty-five. Can you remember much about the Catacombs within the Hellfire Caves?"

"Sorry, I don't. What will she look like?" He pulled out the footstool from beneath the desk, then sat next to me.

"I have no doubt she'll have my eyes. I wrote that she was the most beautiful vampire that had ever existed. I'm sure Varik wouldn't have settled for anything less." And I really did want him to be happy.

"What happens if she kills an innocent person? You won't be able to forgive yourself," he cautioned me in his fatherly tone. He may not be my father by blood, but he is the only dad I'd ever choose.

"So, technically, she doesn't exist yet. If she has killed innocent people in her story, which she may have done to survive, it's yet to happen. I believe I have found a way around that issue, though." I pointed to a paragraph for him to read. "And if Varik gets to her in time, it won't be a problem anyway."

"Will Varik be able to control her?"

I raised my brow. "Control? I'll be honest. Originally, Varik wanted a few vampires, and I did say he'd have to keep them under control, but I want Harper to have her own mind. If Varik is happy to feed on the depraved, then why wouldn't she be?"

"This is exactly why you need to think things through.

What happens when she develops her own mind, as all your characters do, and wants to feed from children, for example?"

"She won't. Varik isn't just happy to feed on the depraved, he's helped out on the *AmberIvy* to save my plesiosaurs. He's a good … person." I almost said 'man', though he is anything but. "And she will be the same."

"Poppet, you and Bowen can be blind to Varik sometimes, perhaps by choice." He put his hand on my shoulder to turn me towards him. "He is a predator who enjoys the hunt. He likes the thrill of hunting down the poachers and enjoys the thrill of luring those paedophiles out."

I wasn't actually blind to that, but that's how we have him. No one is perfect. Although, in comparison to those he chose to feed on, he was. And yet I couldn't stop myself from defending him. "He hunts them down because they're bad people."

He shook his head. "Either way, he does what he does."

"And either way, I can't deny him. His female might even calm him down a bit."

He tutted. "She won't. Where will they live?"

"Varik is still in my old flat, so I assume he'll take her there."

Before David had died, he'd left me his home in his will. After Ivy broke Bowen's leg we had to move in there; my top-floor flat was no good for his recovery. I took my flat off the market when Varik not only walked into my life but also decided to remain in it. He needed a place to stay. I told my old neighbour Sally that I had rented my flat to a man who worked nights. She was extremely anxious at first. Not that I could blame her. I told her not to disturb him during the day, and told Varik not to smile at her under any circumstances. So far, it had worked out well.

David didn't look convinced. "And if Sally ever found out what he was? What about your other neighbours?"

All this started because of the neighbours who lived in our building. They were the scum of the earth, playing loud music all night and vandalising the communal hallway. Worst of all, they were the previous owners of Goodboy. They might have made our life hell, but what they did to him was unforgivable.

"Sally won't care what he is. She's just grateful to have a quiet neighbour."

He laughed at my reply, then sobered. "What about Gary?"

Ah, Gary. He was good to me, and he was my friend. When Ivy left the Inner Temple, she wanted to remain close to me without me noticing. Gary lived in a flat below me, opposite the scumbag neighbours. When she knocked on his door, he let her in, thinking it was me. What happened after that was something I could never forgive myself for. To this day, I will never know how Gary survived; mentally, he hadn't. Of course, the police didn't believe a word of it when he told them a vampire fed from him; who would? I promised myself that I would tell him the truth if he ever asked me about it. I knew he knew I was somehow connected to it.

"Sally told me he stayed with his brother until his flat sold," I explained.

David was about to say something when the bell above the door rang as a customer walked through.

"Good morning," I said, and so did David, out of habit.

People couldn't see him unless he chose to be seen, but if he picked up a book or moved something, they could see the object. We found that out the hard way, and now my customers believed my shop was haunted. I hoped it would make us busier, but apparently, that only worked for pubs and hotels.

I carried on speaking to David in front of the customer, who would shortly come to the conclusion that I had lost my marbles. I should, but never did, get embarrassed. Who cares about what others think when you have everything you ever wanted?

"I still think you should speak to Bowen. Don't keep secrets from him. You two are above that," David chided.

"Okay, I will. I just don't want to upset him."

"I know you don't, but it will be worse when he gets back then finds out."

"You're right—"

"Sorry, did you say something?" my customer asked.

"Just talking to my dog," I answered, then I picked Missy up to sit on my lap.

My customer accepted this with a tight-lipped smile and a nod, then they went back to browsing.

"Did you want to read it, then?" I nodded towards my laptop, then smirked. "It's basically a vampire-romance story – your favourite."

David rolled his eyes, then he motioned for me to move the laptop in his direction.

***

As predicted, David hated my story. After we closed the shop, we walked back to mine and talked about everything and nothing, as we have always done.

He hugged me goodbye at the door and told me he'd be back on the *AmberIvy*. "Speak to Bowen," he told me one last time before he left.

Both Missy and I watched him walk away into nothingness.

"Come on then, Missy, let's get you some food," I said while I opened my door.

When David lived here, you couldn't see the carpet. There were piles of books all over the place. Without his books and Bowen, my home was empty. I picked up one of Bowen's hoodies from the hook, brought it to my face and then put it on.

I knew I wouldn't be able to eat until I had spoken to him, and I didn't want to wait in case he phoned me while I was unprepared. I needed to get this over and done with. I picked up my landline phone and dialled the *AmberIvy*'s landline, if you could call it that. Mobile phones weren't always reliable at sea.

The landline beeps instead of making the usual ringing tone. My heart pounded. *Is it hot in here?*

"Yep. Hello."

"Harry, it's Zoe. Is Bowen free?"

"Let me find out." He then called out to Rory, his first mate, telling him to find Bowen. "How are you?"

"I'm good. How's it been so far?" I dreaded his answer. If he told me another one of my plesiosaurs had been slaughtered, I would lose another night of sleep.

"We still haven't located the plesiosaurs, but that doesn't mean they're not out there. If we can't find them, then neither can the poachers. We're tailing a ship as we speak, actually."

"What's the ship called?"

"There's no markings or flags, but it looks military ... Bowen's here. Bye, Zoe."

"Bye."

He passed the phone over to Bowen.

"Hey, sweetheart. I was just coming up to phone you. How was your day?" Bowen asked.

The *AmberIvy*'s only nautical telephone was on the ship's bridge, so I knew our conversation might not be private. I was tempted to not follow through with my confession, but the sound of his voice made me crumble. "I'm writing a story about a female vampire who was orphaned after her parents died in battle. Her name is Harper. I'm so sorry," I blurted out. Bloody hell, my voice couldn't have gushed with more guilt, even if I tried.

"*What? Why? Couldn't you have waited until I got back? What did David say about it?*" he shouted.

I was about to answer when he said, "Varik put you up to this, didn't he? I told that prick to make sure you didn't write."

"Hey, wait. You told him to make sure I didn't write? I'm not banned from writing. You have no right to ban me. I know what I'm doing." My anger flared from nought to a hundred.

"Do you? Did Varik convince you to do it, or did you both plan to do this before I boarded? Was that why he didn't join us?"

"No, it wasn't like that; you know that. I wanted Varik to go with you, I promise. He wanted a female. I couldn't say no … At first I did, but then I realised how much I missed writing. I wanted to do it and to do it for Varik. Why should I be made to feel like this? I haven't done anything wrong."

"Does David know?"

"He read it for the first time today."

"And what did he say about it?"

He had said my story was complete shit, but I knew that wasn't what Bowen meant. "We both agreed that she'd feed the same way Varik does. She will be Varik's responsibility."

"What if she's like Ivy? What if she can't be controlled?"

Here we go again. I can't believe he and David have said the same thing. They both had zero compassion for Ivy. I sort of understood why, as she had killed one and broke the leg of the other. But they were also my loved ones she had done that to. If anyone couldn't forgive her, it should have been me. Maybe it was time I sat them down and told them how I really felt about it. I had named the ship they were on after her, but they never did ask why. Maybe they had just assumed I did it to be reminded of my mistakes, which was partly true, I suppose.

"Harper and Ivy are completely different. Ivy was acting out of desperation and revenge. Harper has nothing to do with the Inner Temple. Varik will show her a better way—"

"*Will he?*" he roared down the phone.

Tears streamed down my cheeks. Bowen had never shouted at me like that before. "I'm sorry, but—"

"We're somewhere off the coast of Iceland; if it's possible, I'll take one of the small boats out to get to shore, and then I'll book a flight back." He sighed heavily down the phone. "I should never have left."

"Please don't do that; it's too dangerous," I begged. "Look, I know what I'm doing. I have this under control."

We both sat there not talking, both perhaps not knowing what to say next without saying something we couldn't take back. I could call him controlling, and he could throw the fact that two people had died in my face. It was then that I realised how irresponsible I was being, and why Bowen had every right to his anger.

"I am sorry," I said finally. Wanting to reassure him, I repeated, "I promise you that none of this was planned behind your back."

"It doesn't change what you've done, Zoe. You said

you're writing a story; does that mean you haven't completed it yet?" He sounded hopeful.

Not that the story needed to be completely finished for my characters to come into existence. "No, I haven't finished it yet, but this isn't just about me. Shouldn't Varik have a female? His existence is lonely, don't you think?"

"He is not lonely."

"How do you know?"

"Because he's … he's Varik. Zoe, I don't want you to write any more, not until I get back, okay? Will you do that for me, sweetheart?" His patronising tone ignited my temper. He had never spoken to me like that before.

"I can't do that. As I said, I have this under control," I snapped.

"Think this through, please."

"I have—"

An alarm shrieked through the phone. The sharpness of it made Missy howl.

"*That's the emergency alarm,*" he shouted to me, then I heard him bellowing over the noise to someone else.

"*What is it?*" I shouted back. A few seconds later, I still hadn't got a reply. "*Bowen?*"

The blood drained from my face, and my fingers became ice. *What's taking so long?* I tried to listen, but I couldn't make out the panicked orders being barked by Captain Harry.

"Zoe, a ship we were tailing has turned around to face us. I'll speak to you when it's over. I love you,"

"I love you too," I said, after he put the phone down.

***

My ear was still ringing while I was in the shower. I tried to convince myself over and over that Bowen and the crew were safe. It wouldn't be the first time the *AmberIvy* had been under attack – both with and without Varik to defend them. *Did Harry say it had been a military ship? They have gone against military ships before; they will be fine.* I had to read so many books about ships to get the *AmberIvy* just right. She was a powerful ship that could sail without sonar detection. Of course, she was now considered an illegal ship. A pirate ship.

Bowen didn't want me to finish Harper's story, but honestly, I needed to now more than ever, to take my mind off things. I needed to write until I fell asleep over the keyboard. It was either that or lie in bed thinking about every bad scenario under the sun. I turned off the water and wrapped myself in a towel, not bothering to look into the mirror. I was quite certain I looked identical to the last time I glanced in it.

Then I heard noises coming from my living room. The distressed whining was too loud to be made by Missy. What could be wrong with Goodboy? I braced myself for his jump when I entered the room, but it never came. He whined and paced nervously. This tugged at my heart and reminded me of when we first met – when he was skin and bone and covered in cigarette burns. But he was a different dog now: he was fearless. So why was he so frightened?

"Hey, Goodboy, what's wrong?" I went down on one knee. "Come here."

He finally came over. He was soaking wet. When he shook his body, water sprayed in my face. It tasted like saltwater.

"Why are you soaking wet, baby boy?" I sang in my dog-friendly voice.

He whined again in response.

It wasn't unusual to be sprayed by the waves, but why

would he be drenched like this? Had he fallen overboard? No, he was too smart for that. Both Bowen and Varik trained him well aboard the ship. Would someone have pushed him off? No, not likely. He would have put up a fight. I had witnessed him rip a vampire's head off. A human would be nothing to him.

My mind raced from one thought to another, but I kept circling back to the same one. I kept on swiping it away only for it to reappear. I couldn't breathe. My lungs started to burn, and I collapsed the rest of the way to the floor. Why couldn't I breathe? I wanted to call out to David, but I couldn't. I crawled to the phone and dialled. There was no dial tone. I slammed the phone down and dialled again, then again. *No, this isn't happening.*

An ice-cold hand covered mine and took the phone from me.

David calmly put it back. He, too, was drenched. His face was filled with anguish and tears were streaming from his eyes.

"Wha … what happened?" I sobbed.

He picked me up and wrapped me tightly in his arms.

"David, is Bowen okay?"

"It happened so quickly," he sniffed. "I tried to stay with him until the end."

"The end of what?" I knew I shouldn't have asked. I tried to cover David's mouth with my hands to stop him from answering.

He moved them gently out of the way. "The *AmberIvy* is gone."

CHAPTER 3

The memory of David being zipped into his body bag flashed through my mind. I was standing in the very spot where it happened. Except it wasn't his face I saw in the bag – it was Bowen's. The numbness I felt back then returned tenfold.

"He's okay, right? He made it off. He's on one of the small boats." I knew I was talking, but I could barely hear my own voice.

My thoughts returned to the night before he left. We were lying in bed, nose to nose, when he said, "I love you more than you will ever know. I will be back before you know it."

David tightened his hold on me, bringing me back to the present. "It was dark. Something struck the hull, maybe a missile. She went down quickly from the starboard side."

"But he got off. He was on the bridge. I was on the phone to him. He would have had a chance."

His body trembled against mine.

Why won't he just tell me he got off? Just tell me that Bowen got off. Tell me he deployed a small boat, and got off. "David!" I pushed him back to look at him. "He got off, right?"

He shook his head, and tears were streaming from his eyes.

He is crying because many of the crew have perished, and I will cry for them too, but Bowen got off. I know he did.

"The ship went down from the starboard side," he repeated. "Everything happened so fast. I held on to him … I held on to his life jacket while he was trying to cut the ropes for the small boat, but a wave separated us. I lost my grip when he went under. I'm sorry, I—"

"No. No. Tell me he got off. You said he was wearing a life jacket." I knew in my heart I was hanging on to false hope, but it was all I had.

"No. He didn't get off. No one did." He wept. "No one did."

"You said it was dark. Maybe he got away and you didn't see?" I pleaded desperately. The walls were closing in, and I no longer had the strength to keep them at bay.

"Zoe, I'm sorry. It happened too fast to launch the small boats. No one made it off alive."

It can't end like this; it just fucking can't. I studied David's eyes, searching for something, anything to contradict what he said. Maybe this was a prank, an evil prank, but one I'd gladly be a part of if it meant Bowen was really okay. Maybe David was just in shock or had lost it.

He cupped my face in his hands. "He is gone."

It was over. I dropped to my knees and screamed until my throat gave out.

***

Every time David went back and forth to the *AmberIvy*, he found himself in the submerged wreckage on the sea bed. He found many of the crew drowned in their cabins, and he told me he had found Captain Harry floating on the bridge along with his first mate (Rory) and second mate (Gemma). My mind flashed back to the night I had created them, which reminded me that I had lost more than I would allow my heart to accept. I kept begging David to go back and look. He agreed, but told me it would be the last time. When he returned, dripping wet with a broken look on his face, I told him that Bowen wasn't on the bridge because he got off, only for him to remind me that Bowen was on deck trying to cut loose a small boat.

My heart and head were at war. I could not let my head win, because if it did, then that would have meant I would never see Bowen again. It would have meant that he died. I couldn't accept that; I didn't want to. I told myself that, without his body, he was technically missing. David didn't watch him die; he didn't watch him take his last breath.

Bile rose from the pit of my empty stomach. I couldn't even comprehend what Bowen had gone through; he must have been so frightened. What if I hadn't been on the phone arguing with him? Would he have had a better chance of survival? Could he have deployed the small boat in time? Why didn't I make him stay? I could have begged him not to go. He was in two minds, so why didn't I convince him to stay? This was my fault.

Varik arrived thirty minutes before sunrise. David sat him down to tell him what had happened; he spoke quietly to spare me more agony, but I couldn't concentrate on their words anyway. Perhaps my mind was protecting me from having to hear it again. After a few minutes, Varik snarled, revealing his demonic teeth, and his eyes glowed with pure hatred. He shouted and punched a hole in my wall. The plaster sprayed around the living room. I have no doubt he would have continued if he hadn't heard the dogs yelping in fear. Then, he kneeled in front of me, took my hand and brushed a kiss on my palm. He said nothing, or maybe he did speak, but it just didn't register with me. David sat beside me and took my other hand.

"Maybe he's treading water somewhere ... maybe he's ..." My voice was hoarse from screaming.

"He's gone, poppet; he's gone," consoled David.

Goosebumps prickled my skin, and my blood chilled. My muscles started to shut down, I felt my body falling and then a black mist clouded my vision.

***

I awoke in my bed with Varik curled up behind me. I was about to scream at him to get out, but then I remembered what happened. He stroked my hair back from my face, which was something Bowen always did. He, or David, had placed Bowen's hoodie over me. The towel I had wrapped around my body was now over my legs. It must have come off when I collapsed. I wanted to inhale Bowen's scent from his hoodie, but I couldn't breathe and my heart's rhythm skipped beats.

"Hush, Watcher. We can bring Bowen back. You know this."

Hope soared, only for it to be diminished seconds later. "He told me he didn't want to be brought back," I croaked. I was uncertain if Varik had heard me.

Goodboy jumped onto my bed to comfort me and perhaps himself. He whined and did what I couldn't: inhaled Bowen's scent from his hoodie.

"There is not a lot he could do if you did."

This made me smile, but only briefly. I could imagine Bowen rolling his eyes if he were here.

"No, Varik," David said from my doorway. "It wasn't what he wanted."

"The Watcher can tell him I made her do it." He shook my shoulder. "Can't you?"

"I can't just lose him; I can't. We were ... we were arguing over the phone before he ... before he..." My voice broke.

I couldn't bring myself to say 'died'. I wasn't ready. I would keep reminding myself that David didn't watch him take his last breath. He was only missing. My mind was clutching on to false hope to protect itself, but I knew it wouldn't last for much longer.

"He knew how much you loved him. If you did argue, it doesn't change what you had." David came into my room to sit on the end of my bed.

He said 'knew' and 'loved' as in the past tense, as in a feeling once felt. *No, I will always love him. How dare he?* "This is your fault. You said to tell him. To tell him I was writing because we were above that." My voice had risen, and I no longer had control of what came out of my mouth. "You did this. If you hadn't told me to tell him, I wouldn't have."

I pushed Varik away from me and got off my bed on shaking legs. I knew I was naked from the hoodie down, but I couldn't give a shit. I pointed my finger at Varik. This was his fault too. "And you. You should have gone with him. Why didn't you go with him? If you had done, he'd still be ... he'd be ..."

"I might not have made it either, and even if I had managed to keep Bowen afloat, he would have frozen to death. Watcher, please, this isn't anyone's fault – not anyone's in this room anyway."

"What do you mean?" I demanded. "Huh? What do you mean?"

David shook his head to silence Varik, who carried on regardless: "The ship that took down the *AmberIvy* is responsible. We will make them pay. We will slaughter them all."

"We don't even know which ship it was, as it had no identification markings, and without a ship of our own, how would we track it down?" David argued. I noticed he didn't condemn Varik wanting revenge.

"We will raise the *AmberIvy* and destroy them all." Varik sat cross-legged on my bed and stroked Goodboy.

"Varik, stop. Give her time to think things through."

"He was my friend. I have a say in this, and I want them to pay with their lives."

"I'm the same, but give her time to grieve."

"Grieve," I mumbled to myself. I allowed both of their voices to drift into the background so that I could hear the voice in my head more clearly. The last time I was grieving, David had died, and I'd still be in mourning if I hadn't resurrected him. I just needed to hold Bowen one more time, and to run my hands through his hair and kiss him. *Where is he now? He believed in the afterlife, but which one? He wasn't religious, or was he? Why don't I know? He said 'heaven', but he never went to church.*

My head pounded with a thousand thoughts fighting for dominance, but one thought came through loud and clear: *Yes, I will create my own afterlife. I will be able to both keep my promise and be with him again. I will create something special – something for us and only us. I will be able to ask for his forgiveness and apologise for our argument. He will be happy. Both David and Goodboy will be able to come and go as they please. I will recreate myself as a being who can cross the boundaries between life and death at will.*

I must keep this to myself for the time being; David won't understand or allow it. Also, it's time to put my abilities to the test and see how powerful I really am; consequences be damned!

But first, there will be payback. I will destroy all those who have ruthlessly hunted down my plesiosaurs and killed my fiancé and crew. It's time people pay for their actions.

Will Bowen forgive me for what I am about to do?

I buried that last thought deep into the back of my mind; it didn't matter now.

***

David insisted on telling Bowen's parents about his death. However, he couldn't use his own name because they already knew he was dead. Bowen had spoken of David and the funeral, and they knew Bowen was now living in David's house with me. David also couldn't confess to being there at the time. How does the sole survivor explain how he got off the ship and found his way back home? This meant that, in the end, he couldn't tell them Bowen had died. Instead, he told them that they'd lost communication and there would be a search and rescue party sent out by both sea and air, which was true because Varik had called it in. There wasn't much sympathy for illegal vessels, but since so many had fought and sunk over the last year – fighting over my plesiosaurs – the Icelandic coastguard was willing to take a look. Not that they would find anything.

Bowen's mum wanted to speak to me, but David told her I was beside myself with worry; I wasn't. I had a plan now, a mission, and I was sitting at my desk, drinking my third coffee, while doing research for it.

I had two things to write about and needed as much information as possible. Firstly, I wanted to find a way to bring down all the poaching vessels and spare the protection fleets. My heart sank when I realised it wouldn't be possible. Varik would have to use all his connections to keep our brethren out of the ocean. If he couldn't, so be it. And what of the fishing boats and cruise liners, the cargo ships and the military? Not my problem. I wondered why I hadn't thought of this before; it would have spared the lives of my plesiosaurs and there would have been no need for Bowen to be at sea. Would he have agreed to my plan? Doubtful.

"Poppet, what are you reading?" David leaned over my shoulder.

"I'm trying to find a way to pay those bastards back," I said absently.

"Yes, Watcher." Varik pushed David out of the way so he could take his place looking over my shoulder. "What are we doing?"

"Zoe, it's too soon. You need to think this through." David pushed Varik back and closed my laptop. He hooked his finger under my chin and turned me to face him. "Why don't we talk about it first?"

"There's no need; I know what I'm doing." I looked into David's eyes, knowing that he would be disappointed in me if he knew exactly what I had planned. "You agree this can't go unanswered."

"I do, but let's discuss it first," he said gently.

"I'll be doing this with or without you. This is going to happen." I reopened my laptop and carried on searching.

"Tell me what you're thinking first, and we'll plan this together."

He wouldn't be assisting with the plans, but I wasn't going to keep anything from him, not from my current story anyway. He simply wouldn't have a say in it. I had already made my mind up; there was no going back. I just needed something big enough and powerful enough to overthrow everything sailing on the seas – all seven of them. I looked down at what was on my screen.

Mosasaurus: no, they were more than likely to eat my plesiosaurs.

Megalodons: nope, same as the previous.

Sirens, which are known for enchanting sailors to crash their ships: no, I wanted something bigger.

Jörmungandr, a serpent that could wrap itself around the world and hold its tail in its mouth: interesting, but not what I was looking for.

Found it.

I turned my laptop towards David and Varik, pointed to the screen, then read out loud: "Even the gods fear it, or so it was believed."

"Feared what?" David asked in disbelief, then he quickly read the rest.

Varik beat him to it. "Watcher, this is it. This will work."

"Oh no! Zoe, no. I'm up for a revival of the *AmberIvy* and her crew, but not that. Poppet, please, let's talk about this first."

"I will be doing both," I said coldly. "And whatever else I see fit."

***

Forty-eight hours after finding out about the sinking of the *AmberIvy*, I had raised her from the seabed and breathed life back into her crew. David took Goodboy with him to the ship to do a headcount. Out of the eighteen crew members, three were unaccounted for: Bowen, Lana and Oscar. If Bowen had been among the dead, then he, too, would have risen. It was then I knew for certain that he hadn't gone down with the ship. The thought of his body being lost at sea brought me to my knees. My heart pounded so wildly that I thought it would explode. Then, that thing happened again where I couldn't breathe. I tried with all my strength to suck air into my lungs before my vision started to close in on itself and I passed out. David had said they were panic attacks. Maybe he was right. Afterwards, my thoughts returned to Bowen; perhaps they always would. *We will be reunited soon, my love; very soon.*

Captain Harry and his crew resumed their search for the ship that took them down; he also confirmed that a missile had struck the hull on the starboard side. So I gave the *AmberIvy* missiles too. I was also surprised to learn that I was able to bring the crew back as they once were: humans, instead of ghosts. I could bring back Bowen as a human too, but not if he was in the middle of the ocean. I couldn't do that only for him to die again in the freezing water. If only he had stayed on the ship. I started to feel like the odds were against me. How could I be this powerful and not have what I wanted most in the world? Maybe I needed more time, or maybe I needed to sleep, but no, I didn't think so. My mind being starved of sleep had been useful in the past.

Both Varik and David were bickering in the background. David wanted to leave things as they were, but Varik, like me, wanted to do more. I wouldn't allow their raised voices to deter me, or let it break my concentration. Once I'd finished with final details on the *AmberIvy's* short story, called 'Retribution', I started a new page and typed …

Even the Gods Fear It
By Zoe Williams

The volcanologist shone the small submarine's lights over the once active volcano. Rumours had been circulating about a new species thriving within it. Some rumours, however, described the new species as a giant, and after the rediscovery of the plesiosaurs, all bets were off. Michael couldn't resist a chance to be a part of the discovery, although marine creatures were not in his field of expertise; submersibles and seamounts were.

"There is movement. Over," Michael said into the radio.

"Describe. Over," his colleague replied.

Michael came in a little closer. Was the seamount moving or was he being dragged along by a rogue current? No, he didn't think so. He decided he was close enough. What was that ...?

"Zoe, please, let's talk this through. I have spoken to Captain Harry, and he's assured me he can and will capture the ship responsible." David pulled my laptop away.

"Do you mind?" I snatched it back and typed:

Michael began to reverse.

"Describe. Over," his colleague repeated.

But he couldn't; he couldn't believe what his eyes were seeing. He reversed even more and tried to keep an open mind. The volcano was called Rosemary Bank, and it was one and a half miles wide. The resting creature was curled up on it. Its tentacles lay lazily, surrounding its bulbous head.

Michael had two choices: call it in or let it live in peace. His mind flashed to that video circulating on social media in which a plesiosaur was being hauled up the side of a ship in a net. It fought for its life for twenty-three minutes before it was shot numerous times.

Whatever this creature was, it was peaceful and deserved to be left in peace – and it would be.

"It's nothing. Over." Michael felt good. He'd done the right thing; he could feel it.

"We have visuals. Over."

What? Of course, the subs recording his investigation. How did that slip his mind ...?

"I can't write with you both hanging over my shoulder," I snapped. I had changed my surname to Bowen's, and I was grateful they hadn't asked me about it.

"Keep going; come on." Varik squeezed my shoulder hard.

"Ow, Varik. It hurts when you do that. Remember you are a lot stronger than I am."

"Sorry, little Watcher. We are a small army going up against the enemy while sitting in your home. I have not experienced this before."

"Neither have we. Poppet, we must take this slow," requested David.

"We will be taking this slow because I cannot write like this. And I know too little about submarines to finish this anyway," I sighed. "I need to do more research."

"I will help you," Varik offered.

"And I know very little about the Kraken." I looked towards David. "Why isn't there much information on it?" He was a sucker for knowledge, as I was. I knew I was taking a gamble in trying to spark his interest. Would he take the bait? I tried again. "Most people believe the Kraken is a Greek myth, but it's not."

"Well, if you hadn't sold all my books in the shop, I'd have the means to find out." He nibbled the bait.

"David, it's a bookshop – as in a place that sells books."

He walked around my desk a few times, contemplating. He obviously wanted to help, but he worried for me. He said it was too soon and that I wouldn't be able to handle the loss of innocent life. I could, though, couldn't I? I'd lost Bowen, and other than him, I couldn't give a shit about anyone else. When the world discovered my Kraken, they wouldn't dare enter the ocean again. You could argue that, in the long run, I'd be saving human lives, although that wasn't my intention. But still, I was going to use that to my advantage.

"I know you're worried. Think of all the lives that will be saved by them not going into the sea," I declared.

"Oh, stop it. Do you think I'm stupid?" He grinned at me. "I can see the upside – believe me, I can. It would solve our problem regarding the plesiosaurs. But I'm warning you: you will not be able to handle this. And I want you to think for a second about what Bowen would say. Would he want this?"

"No, he wouldn't, but he's not going through what I am." I got up to make another coffee.

"Would he be as ruthless as you? And do the same if he were in your shoes?"

"Ruthless?" I repeated. *Is that what he thinks of me?*

"Bowen could be quite ruthless when he needed to be," Varik said, looking up from his phone. A phone Bowen had bought for him. "We sank a lot of ships during our time at sea, and this was sometimes done on his command. He did what he had to do. I believe he'd be just as ruthless where the Watcher is concerned."

David said nothing, but maybe he agreed with Varik. He, too, had witnessed ships going down while he was aboard the *AmberIvy*. Hearing Varik say that Bowen would be as ruthless regarding me as he had been at sea warmed my chilled heart. It also renewed my resolve. My plan would not be derailed.

I went to put a spoonful of coffee in my cup. Shit, there wasn't much left, which meant I would have to leave the house soon.

"I need some time alone." I stood before David while the kettle boiled. "What shall I do about the shop?" It hurt me to ask, given the circumstances.

"The shop will still be there when you're ready to come back. Come here." He pulled me into a tight hug and kissed the top of my head. "Why don't you turn the kettle off and get some sleep? You'll feel better, and maybe you'll feel differently about all this."

I knew I wouldn't, but I thought that maybe I should try to rest. "Okay. What time is it?"

"It doesn't matter." He stood behind me, put both his hands on my shoulders and then led me to the bedroom. "Off you go, poppet; sleep well."

***

My bed was too big again. Since I had moved out at eighteen, I had always slept in a double bed. I hated it because I never knew which side to sleep on. It took up too much room, and washing the large duvet covers every week had become a chore. I would often lie in it, wide awake, and would tell myself that when the time came to buy a new bed, I'd get a single one. I then had a new set of anxieties about how I'd get rid of the old bed. *Does the company who delivers the new bed take the old one away? If not, how does one bin a bed? What would I do with the large duvet covers? Do you just throw them in the ordinary bin?* How something so trivial could prevent one from sleeping was beyond me.

However, when Bowen came into my life, my bed became the right size, and my weird bed anxieties went away. I would not allow them to return.

My laptop lay atop a pillow on my lap. I needed a break from the Kraken story, but I also needed to keep my mind busy. Sleep wouldn't come to me anyway.

My first vampire-romance short story was almost done. With everything that had happened, I was still eager for Varik to meet Harper. He deserved to have what I had – what I still have – with Bowen.

When I started to outline my afterlife story in my mind, I couldn't help but think of the things I might have to leave behind. I still needed to find a way to recreate myself and to be able to cross the boundaries at will. If I couldn't, I would never see Varik again. I couldn't leave him behind. If it does come to that, maybe he and Harper could take this house and the shop when I go? I had a lot to think about and decisions to make.

Until then, payback was still due. I imagined what the Kraken's first attack would look like. It played out in my mind, as if I was watching a film. It was to be against the ships and submarines that aggressively disturb it. Again, it was to be done in the name of scientific research. And that is what would happen. I knew while I was writing the plesiosaur story for Bowen that they would be hunted down. But did it happen because I wrote that it would? No. We fear what we don't understand, or we try to break its spirit into submission. Humans can't stand the thought of being inferior. It's strange, though, because that never seemed to bother me. I believed my plesiosaurs would have been hunted regardless of the storyline's direction. If I wrote about how the world came together to protect and leave them in peace, perhaps my story wouldn't have come into existence. Either way, I would be putting my theory to the test, already knowing the outcome; human nature was so predictable.

The word 'human' lingered in my thoughts. *Am I one?*

I sighed; I always found myself going around in circles when I contemplated my own existence.

Am I a human? I asked myself again. *No, I am the Watcher.*

Excitement and fear trembled through my body. Not only was I about to discover just how powerful I was but the rest of the world would too.

CHAPTER 4

For the last two days, my phone had rung non-stop; it was Bowen's mum, Fiona Williams, and she wanted to know what had happened to her son. What was I supposed to say to her? I couldn't tell her the truth. I couldn't even accept the truth myself. I wondered what would happen when the *AmberIvy* was discovered, and Bowen was not on board. I decided to send her a message. My hands shook while I typed. It is always easier to lie over a text than over the phone, and yet I was able to keep the message brief and honest. I said that I was devastated and wasn't able to talk. I also gave her Varik's mobile number, telling her he knew more about the search than I did. Then I switched it off and lay back on my bed. My eyes slammed shut, reminding me of how tired I was. I sat back up and took a gulp of cold coffee. I was finally ready to write my afterlife story, and I needed a clear mind to do so, but the thought of Fiona wouldn't fade from my mind. I couldn't deal with the guilt of me seeing Bowen again when she could not.

She had been so lovely to me; his whole family had made me feel nothing but welcome. My heart dropped. To be able to succeed in my afterlife story, I would have to numb myself to the guilt. I would have to build mental walls around it.

I could feel myself drifting off when I heard Varik's phone ringing from the living room. He had stayed behind to help me with the dogs while David came and went from the *AmberIvy*. I tried to listen to what he was saying, but I couldn't. I was about to get up when the muffled conversation stopped.

A few moments later, Varik knocked on my door as he walked through. "Fiona rang me. I told her that I'd phone her back when I knew more."

"Okay, thank you. I can't deal with it right now." Saying, "deal with it," rather than, "deal with her," brought tears to my eyes. I didn't mean it like that. She was going through the same hell I was. Or perhaps her plight was far worse, considering I knew the truth and she didn't.

He came over, moved my laptop aside and sat in its place on my bed. "I have also spoken to Captain Harry. He said he relocated the ship that took them down. It's now at the bottom of the ocean."

"That was fast," was all I could mumble.

He grinned, then looked down. "Doesn't change anything, does it?"

"No, it doesn't." It really didn't. Everybody wants revenge when they're wronged, but in reality, it never truly consoles you. Yet, the *AmberIvy*'s sinking could not go unanswered. People had to pay for their actions.

"David will want me to stop now and move on. I'm not ready," I slurred. I was shaking a little too, with light tremors vibrating throughout my body. My body was also begging my mind for sleep. If I didn't comply soon, it would start to shut down, and the choice would be taken from me.

"Neither am I. Where have you got to in your Kraken story?"

"It's complete." I yawned.

He raised his eyebrows at this. "Really?"

In the last seventy-two hours, I had left my room for only three reasons: to let Missy out for the toilet, for me to go to the toilet, and for me to grab a kettle, mug, coffee and a carton of Bowen's oat milk. Having it all on my side table had been handy.

"I may need to revise it over time, but I wanted to try something out," I explained.

"What was that?"

"My plesiosaurs are still being hunted to this day. Were they being hunted because I wrote about them being hunted or because that's human nature? I wanted to know for certain. So far, my Kraken has just been discovered, nothing more. Let's see what happens." My eyes were closed as I spoke.

"I think we both know what will happen."

"We do. I also finished Harper's story." I forced my eyes open to see his smile. There wasn't one. Why wasn't he pleased?

"Little Watcher." He moved up the bed and took my hand. "She can wait. I will stand by your side until I feel you are well enough to stand by yourself."

Tears streamed down my face. He owed me nothing. If anything, he should despise me for trapping him and Goodboy in the Inner Temple for twenty-eight years. When I asked him why he never held it against me – although, at the time, I was afraid to ask – he had simply said, "I wouldn't be here if not for you."

"I'll be okay," I said with a sniff.

"Have you seen the state you are in?" He gave me a tight-lipped smile.

I smiled back, or rather I thought I did. I felt so weak.

"Come on." He whipped my pillow out from under my head and pushed me back. "You will sleep now."

"I need to start a new story." I started to sit back up.

He pushed me back down. "Do you? Start it tomorrow."

"I need to—"

"Do as I say, Watcher, or I will knock you out."

I tried to smile at the empty threat.

He pulled my duvet up to my shoulders, then called for both the dogs to come to bed. After they bounded through the door, he turned off the light. Even though it was pitch-black, I could still feel Varik's presence. Once I had felt the bed dip down to accommodate his weight, I allowed sleep to consume me.

***

The walk to work was an ordeal. My muscles ached, and I was still extremely tired. It didn't help that Missy chose this morning, of all mornings, to sniff every inch of ground. I couldn't blame her; she hadn't been walked in a while, and David had been too busy aboard the *AmberIvy* to do it.

Varik hissed, "Goodboy doesn't do that."

"Yes, he does. He's doing it right now." Goodboy was busy sniffing at nothing in particular. "You don't notice as much because he doesn't need a lead."

"Take her lead off, then," he spat.

"No, she could get hit by a car."

We both looked around. There were no cars at this time in the morning. I was up at the devil's hour, and we left shortly after. We needed to get to the shop before the sun rose, and I wanted to get out of the house. I needed to find out as much information about the afterlife as possible. Hopefully, the book I was after was in there.

"Okay, but if you see a car, get to her quickly." I leaned down and unclipped the lead. I was expecting her to run around like a loon, but she just continued to sniff the ground.

"If you had written us into a story where we could teleport, we wouldn't be having this issue," he snapped at me.

I laughed unexpectedly, then sobered instantly, feeling guilty for it. "When we get to the shop, I want to tell you something about what I want to write next. David won't approve, but I have to do this. I can't not see Bowen again, and after sleeping on it, paying back those arseholes will never be enough."

"I understand. So you will be bringing him back then?"

"No, it's not what he wanted," I looked back to make sure Missy was still following us. "What he wanted was an afterlife."

***

The walk to the shop took even longer than expected because Missy decided to keep running off every time I bent down to put the lead back on. In the end, Varik just snatched her up and carried her the rest of the way. He acted as if he was pissed off with her, but I could see him massaging her chest while she was cradled in his arms.

"The afterlife is another realm, right?" he asked as we walked through the door.

I locked it and made a mental note to keep the blinds

down. "I'm not completely sure, if I'm honest. You could call it that, I suppose. It has many different names and means different things to people. It depends on whom you ask."

"Why did Bowen want that?" He frowned and smirked at the same time.

"The afterlife is a place you go to be reunited with your loved ones after you die. My plan was to create one for us, but it might not necessarily mean his family will one day be able to join him. That's why I need to do as much research as possible," I sighed. "Maybe we could find the one he went to, so that I can travel to it or join it?"

"Your plan is to join him? In the afterlife – as in after your life ends?"

I didn't answer. It was the first time I had said it out loud. I had no intention of ending my life, but I needed to be like Goodboy and David, so I could cross the boundaries and search for him. I couldn't ask David to search for him, for two reasons: firstly, he'd get suspicious and ask too many questions; and secondly, because I already knew he couldn't access the afterlife. If he could, he hadn't mentioned anything about it to me; he was, after all, my version of a ghost. This meant I would have to become something entirely different. My head was starting to pound.

He shook his head. "I don't like the sound of it. Maybe David should know what you're planning?"

"No. Do not tell David. Anyway, we're just doing research today."

"We will think of something else. Why don't we just bring him back? I'm happy to take the blame." He grinned at me.

"We can't do that … if all else fails, maybe. If we can find another way, we'll go for it. But first, we need to find out as much as we can, and who knows? I might even be able to link a gateway from the living realm to an actual afterlife. Or I could link them all together, meaning he wouldn't be separated from his family when they die."

Varik took a few seconds to answer, then he clapped his hands together. "Where do we start?"

"There's a spiritual section over there." I pointed to the back of the shop, then I walked into the staffroom to make a coffee. I felt disheartened before we'd even begun and knew I hadn't really thought this through, but I would prevail. What other choice did I have?

***

"Valhalla sounds great," Varik said, as if we were choosing a film.

"Tell me more about it?" It did sound pretty cool, to be fair to him.

"It says it's the hall of the slain, a majestic hall located in Asgard. Ruled by a god called Odin. Warriors who die in combat travel to Valhalla upon their death … blah, blah, blah … Here." He shoved the book in my face. "They are reunited with fellow warriors and feast on a boar that is slaughtered daily and made whole again every evening."

"Bowen may have died fighting, but his family may not when their time comes. Also, he didn't eat meat, so that's no good." My stomach rumbled at the mention of food. "Would you mind looking after the shop while I grab an early lunch?"

"I can do that, no problem." His face dropped, then he gave me a thunderous death stare because he knew what I was about to say next.

"Remember—"

"Don't smile at the customers."

***

Standing in Bowen's favourite baguette shop made me numb. He got on great with the staff here, and the thought of them asking me how he was flashed through my mind. I lost my appetite and left the shop before they even noticed me in the queue. With no other destination in mind, I headed back. A customer stumbled out of the bookshop's door and tripped over his own feet. He snatched up his bag and ran off down the street. Great. Another customer who wouldn't be returning. At least no one would believe him, and if they did, they'd hopefully just think Varik was a weirdo who'd filed his own teeth into points. Either way, I wouldn't be scolding Varik for smiling at him; I didn't have the energy.

I opened the door, expecting to see him sitting at the desk. But where was he?

"Varik," I called out. Only Missy greeted me. "Varik?"

"*Over here,*" David shouted from the back of the shop.

I was unable to move, my heart pounded wildly in my chest. I rounded a bookcase and saw them. They both appeared to be in the aftermath of a heated argument.

"What's this about afterlives and joining one or creating one? *Have you lost your mind?*" David demanded.

My body trembled. Even Varik took a step back. David had never shouted at me like this before, and yet it was the look he gave me that cut the deepest.

"I … Umm … I'm sorry," I mumbled.

David glared at me. "Sorry, for what? Your stupidity or for keeping this from me?"

"Both," I whispered, then I looked at Varik accusingly.

"Watcher, I'm with you all the way on discovering your powers and bringing Bowen back, but the afterlife, to me, didn't sound right." Varik stepped closer to me. "In order to join any afterlife, you would have to die first. Even if you did do that, you wouldn't gain entrance. According to these books, you have to be a believer."

I went down onto my knees and wept. I knew deep down that I couldn't pull this off. I knew I could create an afterlife, but it wouldn't be real; just my version of one. *And what would Bowen think of our afterlife with just us two in it anyway? What would we do all day? Where would we live, sleep and eat? Would we eventually run out of things to talk about? He's gone. I need to accept that he's gone, but ...*

"I just can't ... I can't not see him again. I will bring him back and ... and Varik will take the blame," I pleaded with David.

"No, it wasn't what he wanted. I know he spoke to you about it. He and I even discussed it. He would often ask me to see if there was an afterlife. I told him that if there was one, I couldn't access it. It frightened him. He loved you so much, Zoe. He was thinking about you when he asked. I know he was."

"He was worried that if he came back like you, we wouldn't be reunited when I died." I sniffed back my tears. "But I told him I could—"

"No, poppet. You will not mess with things that you do not understand, or believe in for that matter."

"Please, I beg you, just hear me out."

"No." He ran his hand down my back. "I will, however, throw you a lifeline. But if it doesn't work, you will move on. Agreed?"

I would try anything; I was desperate and thankful for David's help. Perhaps I should have discussed this with him. "I can't agree to that, but if you have an idea, tell me ... please."

He shook his head while he walked to the door. He

locked it, then took a seat behind his desk. Fond memories flooded throughout me. David hadn't sat behind the desk since he handed me the keys; he wanted me to feel as if it were my shop.

"Has Varik told you we took down the ship that sank ours?" he asked.

I nodded.

"I've been talking to the crew. I can hardly believe they were resurrected to their former selves. Well ... sort of."

"You mean not ghosts; I already know that." I frowned. "Sort of?"

"Yeah, sort of. Anyway, I asked them what they remembered after their deaths. They didn't, the same as me. One minute I was in my living room, and the next, I'm walking back into my ... your bookshop. Except, for them, it was different."

"What do you mean?"

"One minute, they were drowning, and the next, they were as before. I don't know: sleeping, eating and whatever else they were up to before the attack. They said it was like waking up from a bad dream."

"Right, okay. So, how can I use that to get Bowen back?" *What's he getting at? Who cares if they thought it was a bad dream?*

"I'm getting to that. Be patient."

"Can we get him back?" Varik demanded.

David huffed, then he looked as if he were silently counting to ten.

But we don't have ten seconds; come on, come on. Why is he wasting time?

"Captain Harry told me that, while they were tailing the poachers, the *Ocean Warriors* was making its way to the *AmberIvy* for supplies. It was close, and the crew were convinced that the *AmberIvy* went down after it received a distress call – which, of course, it did. After Captain Harry made contact, they believed they were mistaken because, let's be honest, what other explanation could there be?" he said sarcastically.

"David, please."

He tutted at me.

I pulled the stool from beneath the desk and sat next to him, as I had done so many times in the past.

He squeezed my hand. "Write a story about the *Ocean Warriors* pulling up three survivors from the sea."

"Yes! Yes. Why didn't I think of that?" Because I didn't know that the *Ocean Warriors* was so close. I stood up and kissed David on the head.

He laughed it off and looked over at Varik, who looked impressed, but only for a moment, and then he frowned. I knew instantly what he was thinking.

"Wait." I paced the room in an attempt to wrap my mind around this. "You said the crew of the *Ocean Warriors* thought the *AmberIvy* went down; they may have been told differently since, but why would they …?" Both my head and heart pounded.

"What reason would they have to pick up three survivors if, in their eyes, the ship didn't go down?" Varik asked David.

"Because they were still en route and would have obeyed the distress call. They would have automatically searched for survivors, regardless. Harry didn't make contact until after I revived the *AmberIvy*," I said to myself.

"Captain Harry had to explain why the communications were down. He told them that a missile struck, scraping the side of the ship, and they had momentarily lost power. He didn't mention Bowen, Lana and Oscar."

Harry's small lie gave me an idea on how I would be writing Bowen back into existence. "*I've got it,*" I screamed. When the ship turned towards them for conflict, Bowen and two other crew members were lowering the small boats in preparation. When the missile struck, it knocked all three over the railing and into the sea. The *Ocean Warriors* came to *AmberIvy*'s aid, only to find three survivors treading water. They were convinced the *AmberIvy* had gone down until Captain Harry made contact a couple of days later.

I could do this. I could do this now and have him back. Everything would be as it should be. I glanced at Varik; he looked relieved.

"I'm happy for you, poppet, but as always, you have only heard what you wanted to hear," said David.

I was too excited to care. All I could think of was holding Bowen close to me and breathing in his unique scent. He had brought me so much comfort and made me smile and laugh every day. How could I ever imagine life without him?

"What didn't the Watcher want to hear?" I heard Varik ask.

"All of the crew, although human, do all have her bright-green eyes. When Bowen comes back, he will technically be one of her characters."

***

My keyboard sounded like a machine gun, apart from the occasional ceasefire every time I misspelled a word. The shop had been closed since lunchtime, but we all stayed behind well into the night. This was apart from Varik, who needed to leave for a couple of hours to feed. This time, he had a 'date' with a man from Witney – our town. I was both sickened and pleased; sickened because it was so close to

59

home and pleased because, by tomorrow, our home town would feel that little bit safer and cleaner.

"Would this be considered time travel?" Varik asked.

I was about to answer when, thankfully, David did. "She's just rewriting the story. You could argue that she's going back in time, I suppose."

I knew very little about time travel, but it got me thinking. Couldn't I just rewrite the story from before Bowen left? If I could go back in time, I definitely would have begged him to stay. But what if I just rewrote that he decided to stay? Nah, that wouldn't have worked; it would have been out of character, and the last thing I wanted to do was to change him. Plus, I had the other two crew members to think of; they, just like Bowen, risked their lives to protect my plesiosaur. Also, crew who were not created and accepted the supernatural were hard to come by.

"Harper is thirty-five years old, but technically, she's only a few days old. I kind of went back in time with that," I said, trying to add a little to the discussion.

"It's different," David stated simply.

I looked up, waiting for him to explain; he never did. Perhaps it was something we could explore when Bowen got back. I went back to typing furiously, then I stopped. Wait, I took a moment to have an in-head debate: when he came back, I would have to stop writing again. My shoulders slumped. So, no, I wouldn't be exploring time travel any time soon. It didn't matter; Bowen came first.

"Need help, little Watcher? If I were writing, I'd raise the stakes and put sharks in the water, while all three of them were waiting for rescue. Bowen was scared of sharks, even the bloody baby ones." Varik smirked, and so did David.

"You're both terrible," I replied with a smile. It felt so good to smile. The first thing I was going to do when I heard from him was to tell his mum. The guilt of that alone was heart-shattering. "Hey, should we call Fiona and tell her he's been found?"

"No, not yet. We need to see if it works first." David was looking over my shoulder, reading what I had written so far.

"It will work." I would write a thousand different stories and spend the rest of my life writing them until it worked.

David gave me a stern look. "Please, wait until we are certain. She's been through enough."

"Okay. Maybe Varik can call her and say we found out today that a friendly ship was heading towards them for supplies. He can tell her we're waiting for a response." That would be the truth and would hopefully offer her some peace. "David, we need to tell her something."

I could see David taking a few seconds to think this through. "Okay," he agreed.

While Varik went off to make the call, David took a seat next to mine and wrapped his arm around me. More tears ran down my cheeks. I really didn't know what I would do without him. He was always there for me.

"I really am sorry for keeping things from you. I just didn't want you to stop me," I explained, sniffing.

"I know you are, and I knew you were up to something anyway. Why do you think I'm helping you? Plus, I want Bowen back just as much as you do," he admitted.

"You do?" That was a stupid question.

He smiled fondly. "Remember when it was just us two against the world? I was thankful every day that you decided to stick with me." His eyes watered. "But now, we are a family of four – or six, I should say. And I can't tell you how delighted I am and how happy I have been lately."

He was right: we are a family now. I should have made

the most of it when we were all in the same room together. I would never take it for granted again.

"I knew you loved Varik too," I teased.

"Sometimes." He rolled his eyes. "I couldn't stand the thought of not having him around, put it that way."

"Harper is waiting – well, she doesn't know he's coming yet. I hope he sticks around after they meet." I really did, and I couldn't wait for her to join our family.

"Poppet, I don't think we could get rid of him even if we tried. And I will be keeping my mind open where Harper is concerned."

We both stood up to hug each other.

"Get rid of who?" Varik scowled, then he smirked. He put his phone back in his pocket. "Fiona called me 'an angel' just now. How about, when this is over, I bugger off and live with her?"

"An angel?" David raised his brows.

"The phone call didn't go as planned. She was crying, so I told her Bowen had been found, to make her stop. No pressure, Watcher; you need to pull this off."

"For fuck's sake," David snapped.

"It's okay; I've got this." I could somehow feel it working already.

"Not for a few more days, you don't. You need to sleep or your story will start to write itself," David reminded me.

Ah, yeah. 'The Inner Temple' was written while I was half-asleep, and my characters had conspired against me. But this was different. Still, what was that niggle I had just felt? Why was I coming over all hot? Had I missed something? But what? I racked my brain for the reason why I would have a niggle. The niggle was trying to warn me about something. I'd written Harper's story while both half-asleep and fully awake. Yet, I had reread what I had written, and it was fine. The *AmberIvy*'s story may have been written in a fit of rage, but I was still semi-awake for that. That left my Kraken story, 'Even the Gods Fear It'. I had a theory, and I wanted to put humanity to the test, knowing full well they'd fail. That wasn't it. I had completed it and reread it. No problem there, so …

"Oh shit!" I declared.

"What?" queried David.

"I need to finish this story now." My adrenaline spiked. "I can't stop until it's complete. As soon as it has worked, we need to alert the *Ocean Warriors* and get Captain Harry to dock. Varik, you need to use all your connections to get all protection fleets out of the sea."

"Poppet, what's going on?"

"The Kraken's awake."

CHAPTER 5

B efore I knew it, the night had given way to the morning. Varik took the dogs home, and I asked David to go to the *AmberIvy* and wait by the radio for a response from the *Ocean Warriors*, and to tell Captain Harry what I had done. I could just imagine Harry's response: it wouldn't be a good one. He was with Bowen when it came to my abilities, and he wasn't at all in Varik's court of appreciation. Although something told me that when the Kraken made its first appearance, most ships would either dock or go on the attack. My plesiosaurs would become old news. Maybe then he'd see the advantages. Plus, he would be getting three crew members back. Hopefully, in time, everyone would come to see it my way. It wasn't like there were any other alternatives, were there?

I could sense someone walking back and forth outside the shop, even though the blinds were still down. I wouldn't be opening the shop today, so I didn't concern myself with it. They'd soon get the message. My eyes were heavy, and my head pounded. I put a spoonful of coffee granules in my mouth, then washed them down with my leftover cold coffee. I had to finish this story. It was almost complete.

A light tap on the window broke my concentration. *Am I expecting a delivery? No, I'm not. They will go away soon.*

Tap. Tap. Tap.

My temper ignited while I sat in the dark, debating what to do: *I can just sit here and ignore it, or I can quickly tell whoever it is that we are closed for the day. It will only take a few seconds. Okay, let's get this over with.*

The person tapped once more while I was opening it. When I saw who it was, my mouth opened and closed.

"Hello, Zoe."

"Ga-Gary."

My beating heart pulled me out of my exhaustion faster than any amount of coffee could have done. I hadn't seen him since David's funeral. His timing couldn't have come at a worse time. I could promise to tell him everything and see if he would come back later. Would he accept that? I doubted it – I probably wouldn't either.

"May I come in?" His demeanour told me he wouldn't be taking no for an answer anyway, despite his polite tone.

"Er, yeah. Er, we're not open today, though."

"Zoe, I am not here to buy a book," he said with a clenched jaw.

He was frightened of me the last time we met, and he had taken a step back when I walked towards him. This morning, he was different. I hadn't met this Gary before. This Gary was deadly serious, and the kindness that had always shown in his eyes was gone. He wore black jeans, a black-and-grey military-style coat, and what looked like a balaclava folded up on top of his head to form a beanie. I could see the two holes in it for his eyes folded against the wool fabric.

"Oh, er. Come—"

He walked through before I could finish and looked around the shop casually. When his eyes landed on my desk, he stared for a while, then he frowned. "Have you been here all night?"

There was a blanket moulded to my chair, and a kettle and other crap spread over the desk, but still, there wasn't enough evidence to suggest that. It didn't matter. I had promised myself I would one day tell him the truth; I owed him that much. So there wouldn't be any lying, and that would start with his first question.

"Yeah, I have," I admitted.

"May I ask why?"

"I'm writing. I started something last night and didn't want to waste any time making my way home."

He frowned, opened his mouth to say something, then paused. Perhaps he wasn't expecting my honesty. "Where did you sleep?" he asked finally.

"I didn't ... I mean I haven't. Not yet."

"You look like you haven't slept in days."

"I haven't," I replied with a yawn. I walked back behind my desk and pulled out the footstool for him to sit down on; he didn't want to. I asked him if he wanted a coffee; he didn't want one.

"I know why you're here. I don't know where to start, so how about you ask, and I'll answer?" I suggested.

"How about I start by telling you that there is a leech living in your old flat – next to Sally, no less. And that *it* comes and goes as *it* pleases from here and David's old home."

Heat crept over my face. Many times, in my mind, I had replayed the conversation I would have to have with

Gary, but I didn't expect him to come out with that. This was going to be more difficult than I expected. "His name is Varik."

"*It* has a name?" he snapped.

My blood boiled. I would not, no matter what Gary had been through, allow him to call Varik '*it*'. He was different from Ivy, and I would make him understand. "He's—"

"Who do you talk to when you're in here or walking home? It looks like you're talking to yourself, but you're not, are you?"

"You've been following me?" I suppose it didn't matter now. "David and a dog called Goodboy. The same dog who used to live opposite you."

"David? He's dead." He slammed his fist against a bookcase. "What shit is this? I'll tell you who you talk to: it's that vampire leech, isn't it? They have the power of invisibility, don't they?"

"No, they don't." I struggled to hide my smirk. Varik definitely wouldn't say no to that power, among many others.

"Why are you smiling?"

I sobered, "No, they do not have the power of invisibility."

"*Liar!*" Gary stood tall and stepped closer. We'd have been nose to nose if he hadn't been a foot taller than me. He was trying to intimidate me, but it was, well, Gary. I laughed inside, but it must have come out on the outside in the form of another smirk.

He gripped my jumper either side of my shoulders and shook me. "Tell me the truth – now."

I did what I hadn't done in a long time and let power hum throughout my body from my core to my hands. I held them up, then pushed him back with my mind. My intention was to do it gently, but he went flying into a bookcase. Books fell from the shelves and scattered around him.

"Gary, I'm sorry. Are you okay?"

He was winded and looked too bewildered to answer, so I took this opportunity to talk. "Look, I really am willing to answer all your questions, and truthfully. Please, if you could just listen to me."

"Wh-what are you?"

"There isn't a name for what I am, not that I know of anyway. I write stories, and they become as real as you and I. I wrote myself into one of my stories once and gave myself the power of telekinesis. Hence, your … fall."

"That's rubbish—"

"I really am telling you the truth. How else do you explain Ivy and Varik's existence?"

He shuddered visibly when I said her name. It was then that all my fury drained away. Gary wanted answers. He may have gone the wrong way about asking, but I could understand that. I could only imagine what it must have been like for him, when he was trapped in his own home being used as Ivy's own personal blood bank.

"Didn't you just somehow become … affiliated with them?"

"No." I shook my head. "They are my creations. You should know that Ivy is dead, by the way. It's just Varik and another vampire called Harper. She doesn't live around here." Yet.

Gary was still on the floor, looking up at me, when I noticed all the tension leave his body. He dragged a leg up and rested his elbow on it with his head in his hands.

"Ivy is dead," he said with a sniff.

I nodded. "Yeah, Goodboy, the dog … you know, bit off her head."

"How did Bowen break his leg? Was it Ivy who killed David?"

He'd been putting two and two together, and we clearly had so much more to discuss than I realised. I was going to tell him everything, but first, I needed to answer his last two questions.

"Yeah, she broke Bowen's leg and killed David. Look, I promise I will answer all your questions, but I'm in the middle of doing something really important. I would ask you to go and come back, but I know you won't, so feel free to wait in here. I'll be an hour or two."

***

Gary watched over my shoulder the whole time I typed. He tried asking the odd question, but I told him to wait. I'd got to the bit in the story where the crew of the *Ocean Warriors* had lifted Bowen on deck for medical treatment, and I wanted to make him as comfortable as possible. Tears fell freely from my eyes when I'd finished. Soon, we'd be together again. The Kraken hadn't made an appearance yet, so we hopefully had time to get him home. All I wanted now was to sleep, but I had Gary to deal with first. This wasn't going to be easy.

"I noticed you were making notes. Are they the questions you wanted to ask me?" I sighed, then switched off my laptop. My eyelids grew heavier, and my body started to tremble again.

"Do you have eyes in the back of your head now, or are you a mind reader?" he asked snidely.

"Neither. You took a pencil and pad from my desk, and I could hear you writing. You have questions, and as I said, I will answer them all." I yawned.

"Why are you writing a story about Bowen?"

"Because four days ... maybe five days ago now, he drowned at sea. I'm rewriting what happened to bring him back."

I saw the disbelief in his eyes and knew this day was going to be long. I offered him a coffee, and this time he accepted. We spoke for over three hours. I started at the beginning with Umbra, a black cat who was one of my first creations. I told him about my plesiosaurs and the *AmberIvy*, and stupidly, I told him about the Kraken. I didn't need to tell him about the latter, but exhaustion hinders one's ability to think before speaking. He had also asked me a few questions I didn't know the answers to, such as why I can do what I do and why all my characters have my eyes. He had doubt in his eyes every time I shrugged my shoulders. I also used this time to apologise, over and over again; he never accepted it, not that I could blame him. When all was said and he'd finally run out of questions, we sat in silence for a while.

"Do you think it's right?" he asked eventually.

"I didn't really believe I could do it at first. I just hated our neighbours so much, and I did it partly out of desperation and partly wishful thinking."

"I wasn't talking about that. What you're doing now, bringing Bowen back, do you think it's right?"

"What other choice do I have?"

"The same choices everyone else gets, which is to grieve and then move on." His snide tone had returned, igniting my anger.

"If everyone could do what I can do, they would." I imitated his snide tone. He was not going to make me feel guilty for this.

"It would be a very crowded planet, wouldn't it? But

just because you can, it still doesn't make it right." He said it as if he wouldn't do the same. What a hypocrite.

"I don't know why I can do what I do. If I can do something good with it, why not?"

"Something good? You created vampires and unleashed them into the world. You bring people back from the dead, and you created those freak-show dinosaurs. And what of that other monster? You're out of control, Zoe." His voice had risen.

Freak-show dinosaurs. Monsters. How fucking dare he! "Why did you come here wearing a balaclava, Gary? Were you going to rough me up? I have nothing to be ashamed of."

"Amber Morris."

Two words, one name. That's all it took to take me back to my lowest point. If making unlimited creations was my superpower, then guilt was definitely my kryptonite.

"This conversation is over. Sally told me you had sold your flat and moved. That was my fault. I will pay back all the moving costs and give you compensation." I sounded devoid of emotion. I waited for the guilt to creep over me, but this time, it didn't.

"What happened to that sweet girl who lived upstair—"

"That sweet girl got sick and tired of being pushed around. You remember what it was like living there. All I wanted to do was sleep, work and write. Three simple fucking asks from life." My voice was hoarse, but nevertheless, the intent was there.

"People go through tough times. We were all going through it together. But what you're doing now, Zoe, it's not natural." He shook his head. "It's wrong."

"It's wrong is it? I had no one to call my own and only one family member. Did you know that I only had David?"

"People lose loved ones all the time; it's a part of life."

"But that doesn't mean it has to be a part of mine."

When he realised he wasn't getting anywhere with this, he tried a different angle. "What about what happened to me? Amber Morris. People are dying every day trying to hunt and save those things in the sea."

Those things. "As I said, I didn't truly know what I was capable of. And as for my plesiosaurs, if they were left in peace and not hunted, then there wouldn't have been any deaths." Humanity was to blame for all those deaths at sea, not me. Why couldn't he see that?

"That leech needs to feed to survive. How many people has *it* killed?"

"His name is Varik," I snapped. "He feeds on paedophiles. The world is a better place thanks to him. Why don't you send him a thank you card?" I didn't need to listen to this shit. I walked to the door.

"So you're the judge, jury and executioner, are you?"

"I am whatever I need to be to protect my family. What's the alternative?"

He cautiously took a step closer towards me, then another. He lifted a hand, intent on putting it on my shoulder, but then thought better of it.

There might be twenty-odd years between us, but we used to have each other's backs. I remembered the time, back at my flat, when my front door got kicked in by the fire services. Not only had Gary called the locksmiths but he had paid too. I would always regret losing him as a friend, and I had mentally prepared myself for his hatred when the truth of what happened was laid bare. But you can't truly prepare yourself for this, not until it happens. I certainly didn't foresee our new feelings towards each other to be mutual. It was fair to say that I don't like to be questioned, but to question my family's existence was intolerable.

"I could help you destroy them, Zoe, and put things right."

"Destroy my family, you mean? Get the fuck out, Gary." I unlocked the door and held it open.

"You can't get away with this." He made no move to leave.

"Why don't you call the police, then? Oh, that's right, you did. Remind me again, how did that go?"

"You bitch." He rushed forwards.

I held my hand out, palm up and raised him a foot off the ground. He struggled pointlessly against my hold. The sheer panic in his eyes should have broken me. It didn't. My family came first, and he wanted me to destroy them, just like that. If he couldn't be reasoned with now, then he would never see it my way: the only way.

I lowered him. "Vampires don't have the ability to become invisible, but they can teleport. All I have to do is call his name."

He was visibly shaking when he rushed out of the door. He went right out into the road and faced me.

"I really am sorry about what has happened to you, I truly am. I think it's best that we stay out of each other's way."

"You can't get away with this," he said again. "Sally has the right to know what her neighbour is."

"Go and tell her then, and anyone else who will listen."

I slammed the door, locked it, and threw the last image of him and his seething death stare to the back of my mind. I had more important things to think about. Bowen was coming home soon. I wanted to clean the house and make it nice for when he came back. I also needed to pop to the shop on the way back home to grab some dog food.

When I finally got to my door, I couldn't even remember the walk home or paying for the dog food. I rummaged through my bag over and over again, looking in every compartment, and I checked my pockets twice before realising my keys were already in my hand. Varik opened my door while my keys were in the lock, and he stepped back to let me through. After forcing myself to greet the dogs enthusiastically, my posture slumped in defeat.

"Have you heard anything from the *AmberIvy* yet?" I asked.

"No, little Watcher." He frowned. "You look like death warmed up, as David always says. Have you finished the story?"

"Thanks, and yeah, I finished it, but I need to sleep now. Will you wake me if you hear anything?" I stumbled back while trying to take my shoe off.

"There's an apple pie in the kitchen. Maybe you should eat it before you go to bed," he said while he helped me out of my other shoe.

My stomach cramped at the mention of food. When was the last time I ate? I thanked Varik, then watched him pick up Missy and nestle back into the sofa with Goodboy. How could anyone call him a leech? Gary just didn't know him the way we did. Even the *AmberIvy*'s crew had nothing but respect and admiration for him. Gary was wrong. He had his reasons, of course, but like all people, you had the good ones and the bad ones. Varik was definitely one of the good ones. He was sweet and considerate, and he baked for me. "You made me an apple pie?"

He frowned, then grinned. "No, I did not make you an apple pie. Sally keeps leaving them for me outside my door. I went home earlier for supplies and picked it up."

"Supplies?"

"Clothes."

"Oh." I yawned.

"That you will need to wash tomorrow. Sally is going away for the week."

"For fuck's sake, Varik. You get her to wash your clothes?"

"She offered." He shrugged.

I couldn't deal with this right now. I took my coat off and hung it on the hook. It fell straight to the floor, which made perfect sense, considering I was now standing in the middle of my living room and nowhere near the door.

Varik looked from my coat to me, and then said quietly, "As a one-off, I could feed you the apple pie." He looked concerned for me, which warmed my heart. Bowen once called Varik a rough diamond with a heart of gold. He was right.

"Nah, I can feed myself, thank you. I also need to tell you something before I go to bed."

***

I leaned my elbow on the table, balanced my head in my left hand and used the other to ram the pie into my mouth. It was heaven. Sally had made me the odd apple pie too; she always put cinnamon in hers, which was something that the shop-bought ones don't usually have. I could actually feel myself waking up a little. My body obviously needed the sugar.

Varik listened intently while I told him about Gary. "Do you want me to kill him?"

"No, not at all." I choked on my mouthful. "It's just Gary. He's upset, and rightly so. No one would believe him anyway, even if he did say something."

"Still, he shouldn't have touched you."

"He didn't hurt me."

"That's not the point, little Watcher. He's just a human; he should know his place."

I slid my hand across the table and held his in mine, then I rubbed the pad of my finger over his forefinger claw. I smiled. "You do realise that I am a human too, and so is Bowen?"

"Are you?" He raised his brow.

"I have often contemplated my own existence. It gives me a headache, if I'm honest, and I'm too tired to go there right now."

I was able to stand briefly before falling back on the chair. My vision, too, was now unreliable. The sugar rush had worn off fast, and my body just couldn't take it any more. Varik got up from the table and helped me up. I thought he was going to help me walk to my room when he scooped his arm behind my knees and lifted me up.

"Thank you," I mumbled.

He carried me into my bedroom and placed me on the bed. "Your dog will need to urinate. I will see to it, then I'll wait by the phone."

I tried to thank him, but my mind was already starting to shut down. My last thoughts were of Bowen.

***

Missy woke me up by jumping all over the bed. Where was Varik? It was the morning so I knew he wouldn't be outside. I slid out of bed to get dressed, then I realised I still had yesterday's clothes on, which was both gross and a bonus. Where was my phone? In my coat pocket. I shuffled out of my room and saw Varik at the door talking to someone. Oh shit. Luckily, it was raining outside, and I had a porch that blocked the light from the front door, but still, standing there must be painful on Varik's eyes.

Why were they here? Did Fiona call them? Had they heard something before us? I hid around the corner to calm my nerves and listened.

"We're just here to follow up a complaint made against Zoe—" said the police officers.

"I heard you the first time. Can you explain to me why writing about vampires, dinosaurs and ghost dogs is a crime? Out of interest, what's the punishment? Beheading, hanging or maybe we could disembowel her? I think she'd enjoy that."

Bloody hell. Did he have to be so cocky?

My nerves subsided when I heard the police officers laugh. I walked up behind Varik and moved him to the side. "Is everything okay?"

"We're very sorry to disturb you, Zoe," apologised the female police officer. She looked at Varik, then back at me. "I can see you're very unwell. We just have a couple of questions and won't keep you long."

"Unwell?"

"Yes, unwell," Varik said. "I explained to them why you couldn't come to the door."

"Oh." I should probably have been offended.

The police officer gave me a sympathetic look. "Gary, someone we all know of, said you were responsible for his … Well, as you know, we haven't arrested the person who—"

"Drank his blood and almost killed him," I finished for her.

"Correct. He tells us you were responsible, or rather that you have information regarding the vamp … the woman who did it," she said, cringing.

The other police officer just shook his head, then looked the other way.

I felt bad because it was obviously the truth, yet the truth was so ridiculous that the police officer couldn't even bring herself to say 'vampire'. I hated to lie or to fool anyone, but what other choice did I have? I would try to be as truthful as possible without sounding as mad as a box of frogs.

"I saw Gary yesterday. I think he's just having a hard time." The truth.

"He shook her. Did he tell you that?" Varik said.

I wasn't happy about Varik dropping him in it, but now the police officers no longer looked embarrassed to be here on a waste-of-time visit. Perhaps changing the conversation to a different direction was for the best.

"Is this true?" the police officer asked.

"It is, but I don't want to file a complaint. As I said, he's just having a hard time." The truth.

They both looked at me with admiration. The guilt I felt from that look made my heart sink. I hated having done this to Gary again. I would never be able to make things right between us at this rate.

My house phone started to ring.

"I have to go." I didn't wait around for their response. I rushed to the phone, picked it up with shaking hands, then dropped it. I picked it back up again. "Hello. Hello, Bowen?" *Please be him.*

"No, poppet; it's me."

CHAPTER 6

The line was choppy, and I could barely recognise David's voice. Every time I said hello, he would say something, but I'd completely miss what it was.

"Pop ... *Ocean* ... contact ..." said David.

"What? Hello," I tried again.

"What did he say?" Varik asked.

I waved him away and covered my other ear with one of my hands to block out background noise.

"Made con ... Kra ..."

"They made contact? What did they say?" It must have been the crew of *Ocean Warriors* informing them that they have three survivors; it had to be.

The line went dead.

"Hello. Hello." I slammed the phone down and redialled. Nothing.

I looked at Varik. "Why would the lines go down?"

"It happens occasionally. It sounds like the *Ocean Warriors* made contact."

He looked hopeful, but I needed solid confirmation. My heart hammered, making me feel nauseated. All I needed to hear was that Bowen was alive, or better yet, hear his voice.

I glanced around my home and waited for David to appear. Missy always sensed he was coming before I did, but she just continued to lick her paw. Why hadn't he come? I tried to reach the *AmberIvy* again. Nothing.

"Goodboy," I called out.

Both Varik and I looked around the room. He didn't come. Then Varik called his name. He wasn't coming, and I wondered why.

"Do you have the number for the *Ocean Warriors*?" I knew he didn't, but I was desperate.

"No, we only made contact via radio. They haven't done a crew rotation in months. I'll try to make contact with the ones on break."

"Yeah, okay. I'll keep trying the phone and see if I can get through. Hopefully, David will be here in a minute." I paused. "What happened to the police officers?"

"They said there was nothing else to discuss and asked how Bowen was getting on."

"Oh shit." How could I have so easily forgotten that they could have been his work colleagues? "With any luck, we won't have to deal with them again."

***

Four hours later, David still hadn't shown up; nor had Goodboy. I was losing my mind to both worry and hope; worry was winning. Between the phone call – which I replayed in my mind – and having the police here this morning, my mind kept going back to one thought: *David said, "Kra"; there are no other words that rhyme with that or finish with anything else other than 'ken'. He must have said, "Kraken." Has it made an appearance? Perhaps not, maybe David was just trying to tell me that they were making their way back before the Kraken got to them.*

Now that I thought about it, that was probably what he meant. If the Kraken had made an appearance, I would have seen it on the news in the same way I had discovered my other creation. I looked in the direction of the TV; it was off. I switched it on and looked for the twenty-four-hour news channel. There was nothing yet. Something like that definitely would have dominated the news; to this day, my plesiosaurs still did.

I could hear Varik talking in my room. His voice was soft, and he spoke slower than usual. He was talking to Fiona Williams. At least we could start telling her everything we knew from then on.

But still, why hadn't David come back? What could have been so important that he had to stay aboard the *AmberIvy*? My anxiety was turning into frustration. He must have known how this would affect me.

I walked into my room while Varik was still on the phone, saying his goodbyes. I could hear Fiona crying on the other end.

"I will call you back in two hours, whether I hear something or not." He paused. "I promise. I will let Zoe know. Bye." He reached over to my bedside table and plugged his phone into the charger. He looked defeated.

"You're good with her. What did she want me to know?" She probably thought I was a selfish cow for not speaking to her. I almost didn't want Varik to answer.

"I told her you hadn't been sleeping. She wanted me to tell you that she's thinking of you."

"Oh," I sobbed. I didn't want to ask about anything

else she might have said; it hurt too much. "Umm ... David would have come by now if he were planning on it. I can't just sit around and do nothing."

"What other choice do we have?" he sighed.

"David's car is still parked in the driveway. Let's drive up to Oban. We'll have a better chance of finding out what's going on, and when they dock, we can drive Bowen home. To his family first, then here." *Please say yes, Varik.*

"I didn't think you drove. Bowen told me you couldn't." He frowned.

"I don't have a licence, because when I was younger, I couldn't afford driving lessons, but I can sort of drive. It's the highway code I know very little about, but I can get us there." Both Bowen and David would have gone mad, but hopefully, Varik didn't know any better. I held my breath until he answered.

"Driving looks easy enough to me. It's an eight-hour drive, so if we leave at dusk, we will have plenty of time."

I released my breath. It wasn't like I could tell him I'd be going regardless. I didn't have a clue how to get there, and David's car didn't have sat nav. When we visited Bowen's parents in Scotland, we drove east. Now, we needed to go west.

"Do you know how to use your phone for directions?" I asked while pulling a large bag from my wardrobe. I would need to pack for Bowen too.

He nodded. "And I will book a place to stay en route if I can't contact a crew member."

"We've got a few hours before we can leave. I'll try David again. I take it you had no luck either?"

"No, not yet. Do you know what I think, little Watcher? I think Goodboy is with Bowen. I think that's why he hasn't answered my calls."

"Do you really think so?" I certainly hoped so.

"I also think Goodboy is a treacherous shit, and when this is over, I will be getting a new dog," he said with a grin.

We both smiled at each other.

I closed the distance between us and hugged him tightly, "Thank you for doing this with me."

He wrapped one arm around my shoulders and cupped my head with one of his hands, holding it to his chest. "I know you refer to our coven as a family, but we are a coven, which means loyalty above all else. Do you understand? And even though Bowen is below our station, we protect our own." He lifted my chin and grinned at me.

I didn't know what he meant, but at the same time, I did. To him, being a part of a coven was more important than family. Maybe he was right. Blood, in my experience, has never been thicker than water.

"Stop it," I said quietly. "You're as fond of him as he is of you."

"I know. He has done much for me. Much more than you have, little Watcher." He gently raked my scalp with his claws.

I faced him. "Oh really? So you're not living rent-free in my old flat?"

He laughed. "I have never *paid* to live somewhere before, and I am not about to start now. It's a ridiculous notion."

I shook my head at him. "Fair point. Come on, let's finish packing."

***

I wanted to leave as early as possible. I offered to guide Varik to the car, but he reminded me that he wouldn't be able to see the directions on his phone. Waiting for the sun to go down was like watching the kettle boil: it always took twice as long.

"The sun's gone down. Let me try David one more time before we leave."

Nothing. Even Varik agreed it was unusual for communications to be down this long. A hideous thought niggled my mind, but I mentally slapped it away.

"Come on, Missy, eat your dinner," I sang in my dog-friendly voice. Why was she eating so slowly? "Come on, baby girl." After she finished, I washed her bowl and packed it away in her bag. We'd have to find a dog-friendly hotel when we got to our destination.

"Ready?" he asked.

"Yeah. Let's go."

I locked my front door while Varik unlocked the car. I got into the driver's side and started to sweat. I really hadn't thought this through, but it was fine, I would learn how to drive on the way. Trying to put the key in the ignition with a trembling hand became its very own quest. Finally, it slipped in. "Shit."

"Why won't it start?" he asked with a tight-lipped smile.

"I have no idea." I tried again.

This time, Varik sniggered.

"This isn't funny. How else can we get up there?" I asked.

"Let me try."

"If it doesn't work for me, it's not just randomly going to work for you."

"Just let me try. We are losing the night."

"Fine."

I got out of the car and went around to the passenger side while Varik scooted over. The engine started before I had a chance to close my door.

"Really?" I snapped. "Okay, let's swap back over."

He smirked, then put his foot down on the accelerator.

"*What are you doing?*" I screamed as we rolled off the drive.

"I am driving. Why? Because you didn't even think to twist the key in the ignition." He laughed loudly while heat crept over my face.

"Prick," I whispered.

He laughed harder. "I have seen Bowen drive many times, so I know what I'm doing."

As we drove through the streets, I relaxed. Even though our wing mirror smashed other wing mirrors off parked cars, he really did seem to know what he was doing. It would get easier once we were on the motorway.

"Here." He passed me his phone. "Directions."

Just as I was about to take the phone, I saw a familiar face in a car driving towards us. "Bloody hell. That was Gary in that car."

"It was?"

"Yeah." I looked out of the rear-view mirror and saw him do a U-turn. "He's following us now."

"There's very little he can do while he is in there and we are in here," he said casually.

"It's weird, though. Do you think he was heading towards my home?"

"Did you want me to pull over so we can ask?" he asked smugly.

"No."

***

It was two hours into the drive when Gary finally gave up. What the hell did he want? Well, I knew what he wanted:

answers. It was how he was trying to get those answers that I didn't understand. Varik couldn't care less about Gary; to him, Gary was just a human, and a problem that could easily be dealt with. Though I wouldn't allow that. But to me, he was a problem that wouldn't be going away any time soon. He couldn't get the justice that he was rightfully owed, which meant he'd have to settle for payback.

I looked behind me to check on Missy, who was fast asleep on the back seat, then I looked at Varik – he was fast asleep too. "Varik, keep your eyes on the road," I snapped.

His eyes flew open. "We're on a straight road; don't panic."

"Please keep your eyes open. David always says that it's the other drivers who cause the accidents. Although, I'm pretty sure *we* are the other drivers in this case."

He grinned widely, showing off his serrated teeth. "I was trying to contact a crew member stationed in Oban; her name is Penny. Will you try again?"

"Yeah, of course." I scrolled through his contacts and wasn't the least surprised that he had more than me. "Found it. She knows what you are, doesn't she?"

"She does indeed."

I called her, and she picked up on the third ring.

"Varik, how are you? Long time, no speak. I heard you weren't aboard the *AmberIvy*. Did they tell you why I couldn't make it? I had bills to pay, so I took a bar job," she explained.

"Pen—"

"Why aren't you with them this time? Harry didn't say, and Bowen said you were looking after the Watcher."

"Pen—"

"What's she like? And why do you have to look after her? Did you hear about the attack? A missile struck the ship, it went down, and everyone died. The Watcher brought them all back. The 'walking dead', I call them now. Bowen, Oscar and Lana went overboard, and she wrote this wild story—"

"Pen—"

"—about how the *Ocean Warriors* found them, and they did—"

"This is the Watcher."

She stopped talking immediately. She knew more than we did, which meant she may have heard from them recently. I quickly asked Varik if she had a radio, and he nodded yes. Hope soared through my heart.

"You just said, 'they did'. Have you heard from Bowen?"

"Oh! Oh, Sorry. I've heard so much about you—"

"Please, Penny, I need to know what you know. When was the last time you heard from the *AmberIvy*?"

"Yes, of course. Two hours ago. They were sailing back north to pick him up. Also, the *Ocean Warriors* is dead in the water – it has no fuel."

Tears streamed from my eyes. They were going back for Bowen; he was coming home.

"Are you still there?" she said.

"I am. Do you know how far away they were or how long it will take them to reach the *Ocean Warriors*?"

Penny giggled down the phone. "They were ten nautical miles away from the *Ocean Warriors* when we spoke. Both ships are on their way home as we speak. You must have been so worried, or perhaps not? I suppose you knew you could bring them back, didn't you? How come some come back as ghosts and others don't? Why is Varik a vampire? Oh, wait, what other dinosaurs are you going to write about?"

Varik said something in the background, which I almost missed.

"That's a lot of questions to answer in one go. Umm, Varik said we can stay at yours," I said.

"Of course, I'd be honoured. How far away are you? I always thought about driving down to meet you once or twice."

"You did? Er, roughly five hours, give or take an hour."

"Ah, that's plenty of time to answer my questions. I have so many—"

Varik leaned across and took the phone, "Penny, the Watcher needs the phone for directions." He ended the call, then passed it back.

I needed to take a few minutes to myself to let everything sink in. The fact that I had been able to pull this off in the first place barely registered. *I had wanted to know what I am capable of, but this is enough. No more wondering and no more pushing my luck.* I almost said to myself, *No more writing.* I smiled; that would never happen. Bowen and I had a lot to talk about when he got back. Yes, *when he got back.* When we next stopped to let Missy out to go to the toilet, I would get Varik to ring Fiona.

"Penny seems really nice," I said after a while. If it were under any other circumstances, I would have looked forward to meeting her.

"I was warned before we met that she'd chew my ears off. I was expecting a demon or possibly a witch with an ear fetish. When this little human introduced herself to me, I realised that I had a lot to learn about your language." He seemed to be smiling at the memory.

"How did she react when she found out what you are?" Some of the crew had been created by me, and some had been hand-picked by Captain Harry and David. Penny was one of those chosen, and I wondered how she had passed the test.

"She said I was cool, then she told me how her grandmother could communicate with the dead. She asked if I could do the same, and then asked me question after question until I threatened to rip out her tongue."

This made me smile; it shouldn't have, but it did. I shifted in my seat to get comfortable and looked straight ahead. The roads were quiet at this time of night – peaceful. The hum of the engine and vibrations seemed to soothe me. My eyelids started to feel heavy, and my shoulders slumped. I hadn't realised how tense I was. I took my shoes off, rotated my feet, and practised my breathing exercises: breath in for five seconds, hold for five seconds, then breathe out for five seconds.

"Sleep, little Watcher; we will be on this road for a while yet."

"Okay. If Missy starts whining, will you stop and let her out for a wee?"

"If Missy starts whining, I'll chuck her out of the fucking window."

I shook my head at him, yawned, then bit by bit, mentally shut my own mind down.

***

When I woke, it was morning. My body felt stiff, but panic soon overrode it. Varik and Missy were nowhere to be seen. I looked out all the windows, trying to get my bearings. Why was I in the back seat? The car was parked in the driveway that belonged to a cottage. Where were we? How did we get here? I looked down at my lap for Varik's phone. There was an unfamiliar blanket on me. I could hear seagulls outside, and I only hoped we had made it to our destination – or at least somewhere close to it.

As I opened my door, I heard rapid footsteps heading in my direction. A redheaded woman clapped her hands together when we locked eyes. Her smile was friendly, and her blue eyes were filled with love. She wore washed-out, ripped jeans and a black t-shirt with a well-known anti-whaling logo printed on it. *This is Penny,* I thought. She couldn't have been much older than twenty. Her looks were a perfect match to her voice on the phone.

"Come in, come in." She motioned with her hands. "Varik is asleep, and Missy is sooo, sooo cute. Varik brought her little bag in, and she's eaten—"

"How did we get here?" I yawned and looked back at David's car. "Where is our car?"

"Your car 'broke down'." She air quoted 'broke down', then rolled her eyes. "Varik rang me, and I met him on the outskirts of Glasgow."

"Our car broke down?" Why hadn't Varik woken me? I vaguely remembered him talking to me through the door on my side. He must have transferred me to Penny's car. I always thought I was a light sleeper.

"Nah, it ran out of petrol. We didn't have time for me to fill up cans and get here before sunrise – we made it back just after. I had to guide Varik into my home." She looked amused.

I smiled back at her. It hadn't even crossed my mind to refuel. I shook my head, then stretched and yawned.

"Varik said it was best to let you rest."

I nodded. I desperately needed to know if she'd heard anything, then I realised she could have missed a call while picking us up. She must have read my thoughts.

"They are still en route. David went home to talk to you. He said you weren't there, so I told him it was because you were here."

"Oh, really? Did he sound angry?" I blushed.

"He did."

"Have you heard from Bowen?" I held my breath. *Please tell me you've heard his voice.*

"David said he's still on board the *Ocean Warriors*. I could try to make contact again. I have to be honest, though – I've not had much luck this morning. The connection has been unreliable."

"Yes; yes, please."

I followed Penny into her home. Wow! She could give David a run for his money when it came to hoarding. I had never seen so many electrical devices in my life, and that included walking into a shop that sold them. On every surface of her home, there were laptops, mobile phones, TVs and radios.

She noticed my eyes darting around the room. "I know, I know – but it's all worth money, broken or not. Varik and Missy are in there." She pointed down the hallway. "Here, come through to my dining room, which I also like to call my communications room." She looked proud when she presented it to me.

"Communications room?" I said absently. The dining room table had been pushed against the wall. It was now home to numerous radios, all neatly placed one on top of another. They all seemed to be emitting noise, from a soft crackle to broken speech.

"My job is to infiltrate ships that have secured their radio feed. It doesn't pay the bills, though."

"This is amazing." My eyes continued to flicker around the room. I was impressed. Just from her efforts alone, she would have saved many of my plesiosaurs.

She pulled out a chair for me and took a seat in hers. She put on a headset, then she went to work flipping switches on and off so fast I couldn't keep up.

"This is Penny, come in. Come in, this is Penny," she said into the microphone. "Oh, I forgot to ask. Do you want a drink?"

"I do, and I need to use your toilet too. May I make myself at home while you carry on?"

She gave me a thumbs up and then went back to work.

I headed for the kitchen. Penny had three kettles in her kitchen. At first, I didn't know which one to use, but then I noticed one didn't have a plug and another didn't have a lid. I filled one that already had a dribble of water in, then ran to the toilet. On the way back, I opened the door to where Varik and Missy were sleeping. She was curled up by his side, and he looked dead. I felt an overwhelming urge to sweep his long fringe from his eyes. As I stepped closer, I noticed how pale he was. When was the last time he had fed? It wasn't long ago. Still, he would soon need to feed again. I was sure Oban had its fair share of creeps for him to choose from.

On the way back to the kitchen, I heard Penny speaking. I rushed back into her communications room, only to find her already standing. She passed me a phone. "Hurry, I don't have a strong connection."

"Bowen?"

"No, it's David. How the bloody hell did you two drive to Scotland?"

"Varik did." Heat spread rapidly over my face.

"Stay where you are. I will come to you." The phone line went dead.

"He's coming here. Will I be able to see him?" Penny almost burst with excitement.

"If he wants you to, you will. He doesn't often. He's supposed to be dead." I smiled. "Haven't you met him?"

"I have been in the same room as him, but I only know that because I've seen other crew members speaking to him."

As she spoke, I felt David's presence behind me.

"Poppet." He wrapped his arms around me and kissed the top of my head.

"Hello, David," Penny said while her eyes darted around the room in my direction, then her eyes widened. "I always wondered what you looked like. I thought you'd be younger."

"Thanks. Nice to meet you properly, Penny." He shook her hand, making her shiver.

"Oh, that felt like pins and needles," she declared.

I couldn't have described it any better myself. I looked at David expectantly. Tears were already forming in my eyes, getting ready to fall. All I needed to hear was that David had heard Bowen's voice.

"I have seen Bowen on the *Ocean Warriors*—"

"You have? How was he? Is he speaking? What did he say?" I grabbed David by his jumper to steady myself.

"He's unconscious—"

"How? That wasn't a part—"

"Zoe!" He shook me. "He's alive. That's all that matters."

"Okay. Yeah, of course. He's alive. You saw him. He's alive." I still couldn't believe I had pulled this off, and I'd soon have him back. "What about the other two – Oscar and Lana?"

"Oscar is in the same shape as Bowen, and Lana is up and about; she took a small boat and is now back on board the *AmberIvy*." He smiled briefly, then his face turned to one of worry. "Varik drove?"

"Yeah, he did. David, over the phone, I heard you say, 'Kra,' and why did it take you so long to come home?"

"I wanted to stay with Bowen for a while. I was hoping to be with him when he woke up." He took the chair that had belonged to me, then he sat facing the radios. "Penny, will you open up all the channels?"

"On it. What am I listening out for?" she said while flipping numerous switches again.

I had no idea what she was doing, yet I felt nothing but admiration for her.

"The Kraken," David said simply.

I stared back at him, but his expression gave nothing away.

"Is that a code word for something …? Nooo," Penny said, looking over her shoulder at me. "You didn't."

I nodded.

"Watcher! My dad's out at sea doing seal-watching tours."

"I'm sorry, Penny; I was just so angry at the time. I thought I'd lost Bowen for good, and I felt useless where my plesiosaurs were concerned."

"I get it," she stated, nodding. "I need to get my dad to safety first before anything else."

"Of course." Other than what happened with Bowen and the *AmberIvy*'s crew, this was the first time I was struck with guilt over my actions.

"What will you say to him?" David asked. "We don't know if there have been any sightings yet; we just heard distress calls over the radio that sounded Kraken related. For example, we heard someone screaming about a giant squid."

"I'll just tell him there's a free bar at the Black Swan. And it doesn't really matter whether there have been any sightings or not, because if she wrote about it, then it is already out there," Penny pondered.

She was right. My adrenaline started to spike. All I had wanted was to bring Bowen home, but in doing so, I could potentially be responsible for his second death. I had to find a way to stop the Kraken, but how?

"David, how far away are they?" My nerves were shot, and I felt like I needed to be sick.

"We had to refuel the *Ocean Warriors* near the Faroe Islands, which took longer than expected. It will take another two to three days, depending on the weather." He rubbed a shaking hand down his face.

"Two to three days." My blood ran cold.

CHAPTER 7

V arik still looked a little pale, and if that wasn't enough evidence to prove he needed to feed, then his foul temper was.

"If you're not getting any bites online, ask Penny if anyone around here has a criminal record." I stepped back when he snapped his teeth at me.

"I already have," he snarled. I did not appreciate the fierce look he gave me, but I would let it slide.

"Varik, my ex-boyfriend was such an arsehole, and he only lives up the road," Penny said, then she smirked without taking her eyes off her laptop.

"Which road?" he queried.

"Penny, I don't think you would really want your ex killed," David replied.

"Wouldn't I? He's the local thug. Of all the crimes he's committed, he's not once been charged. Some people just know how to play the system, I guess." She spoke without a care in the world.

I was really starting to like her. Although, it wasn't lost on me that she, too, could play the system. The difference was that she wasn't doing this for herself or greed; as she had said before, it didn't pay the bills.

"What crimes has he committed?" David asked.

"It doesn't matter," I said. "Varik needs to feed." He came first, not some local thug, I wanted to say.

"Not like that, poppet." He looked at Penny, "There's a website that logs all the child sex offenders and rapists living in your local area."

"Yeah, there is, but only the police can access it," I reminded him.

Penny whipped around and pulled a different laptop from a shelf above the radios. It looked like a homemade one to me. I glanced around her home again, then I finally understood why she kept all those broken appliances. She pulled a hairband from her wrist, scraped her long auburn hair into a ponytail and concentrated on her new task. It sounded like torrential rain as she pounded the keyboard. I looked from David to Varik. They both appeared smug.

"What?" I frowned at them. Then it dawned on me. "Can she?"

"She'll find it." David looked at Penny with pride.

Yeah, I could see why she had been chosen now, and it wasn't just because she could handle the supernatural. She was an absolute asset.

***

Penny found what she was looking for in eight minutes. Eight!

"That's amazing ... I meant that you found the website so fast, not ..." That there were so many names and addresses in her local area, which Varik had to write down quickly so she could disconnect from the database. No, that part was depressing.

"Yeah, wish I had done it sooner. It's fair to say that I won't be serving these monsters at the pub from now on." She looked as angry as I felt when I first realised how many predators were out there and living so close.

"Penny, with Varik here, you won't have to worry about them walking into your pub anytime soon," David said simply. "Poppet, I'm going to wait with Bowen. You three stay here and listen out for anything out of the ordinary."

"We will. David, when Bowen wakes up, tell him … tell him …" *Well, shit, where do I start? From the beginning, I suppose.* "Tell him—"

"Poppet, I will, and I'm sure he will understand." He gave me a knowing smile, then he pulled me in and kissed the top of my head before his presence dematerialised to nothing.

"*Whoa!*" Penny roared. "Watcher, when I die, I want to come back like him."

***

We hadn't heard anything from the *AmberIvy* or *Ocean Warriors* all day. Penny said there were a few more distress calls than usual, but nothing to suggest a mythical creature was the cause. I was thankful that the day had gone by fast. It was always better for my nerves when time didn't stand still.

Varik was finally able to leave the house to feed.

Penny made me laugh when she looked at me and said, "Are you hungry?" and then picked up her phone to order two bags of chips from the local chippy.

They were good; I could quite easily have eaten two bags to myself. She had also plonked a couple of beers on the table. I eyed mine cautiously. Alcohol was a sure thing to help me sleep, which is why I didn't drink it much. I didn't want to become reliant on it.

While we drank and ate, she asked me what felt like a thousand questions. I tried my best to answer them all, but the truth was that I didn't know some of the answers myself. A combination of her questions and the beer made my eyelids grow heavy, but I fought against it. I was, after all, the queen of the sleepless. I would not sleep until I heard from Bowen.

I asked Penny if she wanted a coffee.

"Nah," she said. "Grab me another beer."

We didn't leave her communications room all night. After three more coffees, I rested my head on my elbow.

The radios crackled to life.

"Watcher." Penny shoved my shoulder. "It's for you."

I grabbed the headset off her. "Hello, hello." My heart thumped wildly when I heard his voice. A beautiful voice that I thought I would never hear again. But he couldn't hear me. "Hello, Bowen." Tears streamed down my face in frustration.

"You need to push that button so he can hear you," Penny explained calmly.

"Bowen, can you hear me?" Now I couldn't hear him. My hands shook.

"Watcher, you need to push that button so he can hear you, then take your finger off so you can hear him. Only one of you can speak at a time. Say, 'Over,' when you are done."

Of course, how could I have forgotten? I took my finger off the button.

"Sweetheart, I'm with David. He's told me everything. Are you okay? Over."

99

"I'm okay; I just want you home. Over." I almost forgot to take my trembling finger off the button.

"Me too. I miss you. Over."

"I miss you too. Bowen, you need to come home quickly. Did David tell you about the Kraken? Over."

"Yes, he did. You will be in a lot of trouble when I get back. Over."

Guilt warmed my blood, not because I'd be in trouble, but because I could almost see Bowen smiling while he said it. He was teasing me. "Are you angry with me? Over." Stupid question.

"I am very angry. I understand why you did it. I also understand why your characters named you the Watcher. We will discuss …" The line crackled. "… back. Over."

"How long …" The crackling got louder. "Over."

Crackling, then, "… hear you. I love you, okay. Over."

"I love you too. Over."

I heard his voice within the static, but I couldn't make it out. "Hello. Over."

"The line has gone dead, sorry." Penny reached for the headset. "I'm surprised they reached us in the first place."

"Did you hear him? Did you?" I hadn't felt this happy since the day he came back from his first three months at sea, and I couldn't wait to wrap my arms around him the same way I had back then.

"I did. It's crazy what you can do." She smiled slyly. "Now, we are friends, aren't we? That means if I die, you will bring me back, yeah?"

I just answered her with a smile.

"Come on, please." She fluttered her eyelashes at me.

With a grin I said, "I'll think about it. I need to sleep now. Will you stay up until Varik gets home?"

"Yeah, no problem. Goodnight." She stretched and yawned in her chair.

"Goodnight, Penny, and thank you for everything."

She nodded.

"Oh, wake me if you hear anything." I left the room, and as I walked down the hallway, I bumped into the walls on either side of it, and my legs were now buckling under my weight. Yet, I couldn't stop smiling.

***

My eyes were closed, even though my mind was wide awake. Every muscle in my body begged for more sleep while I lay back on Penny's sofa. I frequently found myself feeling this way. I just wanted to replay every word Bowen had said. He said he understood why I was called the Watcher. I knew he had asked Captain Harry, Varik and David. Now he knew why. I have no doubt that he could feel me watching him while he was being rescued by the *Ocean Warriors'* crew or felt me watching while the crew made him comfortable. I guess it was a two-way street; if I could see my characters so clearly in my mind while I wrote about them, then it only made sense for them to feel my presence.

I had purposely written a detailed description of his beautiful, pale-brown eyes. My heart sank then, and again now, because I knew it wouldn't work. I had already tried with David's story. His once blue eyes were now green. I had spent much time trying to figure out why, but nothing obvious stood out. Maybe it was something as simple as the stories were being told through my eyes. *Still, it doesn't matter what colour Bowen's eyes are now, I'll have him back in any way and in any form I could,* I thought.

I finally dragged myself off the sofa when I thought of Missy. She would be needing to go for a walk. When David's car ran out of fuel and Penny had to pick us up, Varik remembered his and Missy's bags, but he forgot about mine and Bowen's. Luckily, my phone was in my pocket. Penny had kindly lent me her clothes. Today, I was wearing worn-out corduroy trousers, which she proudly said had come from a charity shop, and a t-shirt with a logo that said "Powered by plants", written below a bright-green dinosaur.

I helped myself to a coffee, then wandered into Penny's communications room. Varik was listening to a distress call over the radio. It may have been in another language, but the urgency with which they spoke was undeniable.

"Where is Penny?" *And where is Missy?* I thought.

"Good morning, Watcher. She took Missy out for a walk." Varik turned in his chair, then motioned me to sit in the other.

"When did they leave? Oh, did Penny tell you I spoke to Bowen last night?"

"She did." He grinned, then sobered. "I tracked down two of the men off the list. One now has a shallow grave in the woods and the other will join him shortly."

"Okay." He wasn't normally this open with me when he shared this kind of information. "Bowen seemed well—"

"While I was tracking them down, I saw a car; that same car drove past me a few times. When I came back, it was parked down the road. He drove off when I went to investigate." Varik told me this in a bored tone, but I could tell it bothered him. He wouldn't have brought it up otherwise.

"He?"

"Gary."

I knew Gary wouldn't be going away anytime soon, and I was concerned about what he had planned. But he didn't pose any real threat – not really. The situation just spooked me more than anything, putting my nerves on edge. I realised he must have been close by when Penny picked us up. Why on earth would he have followed us all the way to Scotland? What was he hoping to achieve? Perhaps I needed to speak to Gary again. A small part of me couldn't help but feel a little sorry for him. This was, after all, my fault. "It's weird and I don't like it, but what can we do about it? He is harmless, I suppose."

Varik just stared at me.

"He is harmless ... Don't you agree?" What was he thinking?

He sighed before he answered, "Little Watcher, you are right: he is harmless, but only because he is a weak human. His weakness means he will have to think of a different way to get revenge. A different way that we might not see coming."

I had come to the conclusion that he wanted payback, but what could he do that he hadn't already tried?

"What are you suggesting?" But I already knew. A single tear rolled down my cheek. If Varik threatened or hurt him, all he would be doing was proving Gary right. I needed to try one last time to make this right between us.

"I will track him down tonight and deal with it."

"No, let me speak to him one more time. I may be able to persuade him to leave us alone ... or if he meets you, and you show no sign of aggression, he may feel differently about your kind."

When Varik grinned, I realised that would never happen. "As you wish. We will waste time by dealing with it your way first, then afterwards, we will deal with it my way. Agreed?"

"Varik, I don't want his blood on my hands." *Even more blood on my hands,* I thought.

***

Both Varik and I listened to a few distress calls over the radio. Most of them were still in different languages, and some were too faint to be heard. But all I wanted was to hear Bowen's voice again. Varik had kept the channel open, although nothing but static came through. I stood abruptly, about to open a curtain, then I quickly remembered Varik's eyes.

"Varik, will you phone Penny? She's been gone for hours. I appreciate her taking Missy out for a long walk, but she's only got little legs; she'll be shattered later."

He passed me his phone. I rang her number several times before I gave up.

"I'm going out for a little wander. I'll see if I can find them." It was the last thing I wanted to do, but at the same time, I couldn't sit around here all day. I remembered her telling me last night that she worked at the Black Swan. I'd start there.

"What if you see Gary?" Varik asked without turning towards me.

"I will … er, ask him to help me find my dog." I grinned.

He shook his head then smirked. "Stay out of his way until the sun goes down."

"Okay." But I wouldn't. It wasn't like Gary could do much to me in public anyway. I had nothing to worry about where he was concerned.

***

Oban was a beautiful town. The people walked around as if they had all the time in the world; the same way the people of Witney did. I instantly felt at home and decided to get another bag of chips from a chippy – hopefully the same one Penny ordered ours from. After I paid with a tenner I had borrowed from her, I walked down to the seafront to find a bench. The beach, if you could call it that, was surrounded by a stone wall. The bench I found was along that wall. I sat and took in the scenery.

Over to my left, I saw the ferry port for the Isle of Mull. To my right, I spotted a big sign advertising seal tours; that was where Penny's dad worked. A little further up the hill, I saw the Black Swan. While I ate my chips, I regretted not grabbing an extra sachet of salt. I headed up the hill to the pub after I finished them. I wasn't sure if Penny had a shift or not, but surely she wouldn't have taken Missy to work with her?

The pub wasn't busy, so I made my way straight to the bar, but there was no one behind it.

"What may I get you?" I jumped at the voice that came from a table behind me. The speaker put his pint down and rushed behind the bar.

"I'm looking for Penny. Is she due anytime soon?"

"She was due over two hours ago. Though that's nothing new." His angry tone was betrayed by his soft features.

"Oh right. Do you know where she could be?"

"No, I don't. If you see her, tell her she's on her last chance."

I acknowledged him with a nod, then I left to find the seal-watching-tour sign back down the hill. There was a notice on the sign saying "Closed due to bad weather conditions". I looked up just as the sun broke through the clouds. The boat, which I assumed was her dad's, was docked and partially covered in a tarp.

I sent Varik a message to ask him to let me know when Penny returned, then I walked back up the hill to the ferry port. There was a pub with a huge front garden on my way to it, and I decided to stop and have a drink. It was totally out of character for me to do so, but I wanted to sit outside. If I chose the right table, I could see all the way down the high street.

My mind felt like a pendulum, continuously swinging from left to right. Something felt off. I was on my second Diet Coke when Varik messaged to ask if I'd seen her. This was getting ridiculous now. If I kept wasting my time out here, I could miss a call from Bowen. I decided to phone Varik.

He answered on the first ring. "Watcher."

"Have you heard anything from David or Bowen?"

"No. I spoke to Captain Harry. He reckons they're nineteen hours away."

"Nineteen." My shoulders slumped; I hadn't realised how tense I was. Then the tension returned. A lot could go wrong in that time.

"I take it you haven't found Penny."

"No, I haven't. I went to her work and she was due" – I looked at my phone for the time – "about four hours ago now. I'm pissed off now. Poor Missy must be frightened."

"Missy will be fine. Are you coming back now?"

"Yeah, I'm on my way." I looked back at the ferry port. The queue of cars waiting to board had grown even longer. "Varik, how often does the ferry leave for the Isle of Mull?"

"Little Watcher, I highly doubt Penny took Missy to Mull." He sniggered down the phone.

"I know. It's just that one hasn't left since I've been sitting here."

"That could mean anything. Walk over and ask why they aren't running."

"Will do."

***

The blaring car horns got louder the closer I got to the ferry port. I had wondered what that noise was while sitting in the pub garden, and now I knew. The queue of cars was also much longer than I'd first thought. I joined the end of the walk-on queue and asked a few people waiting why there was a delay. The first person I asked snapped at me; so did the second and third. They all said something along the lines of, "We're not being told a thing."

I decided to head to the front of the queue, as maybe there was a staff member at the front.

"*Hey, you! No pushing in,*" someone standing in line shouted.

"I work here. I will find out what's going on, then come back," I said mechanically.

"You tell them to get their arses into gear."

"Will do."

A few of the others in front of me heard what I said and moved aside so I could squeeze through.

There were a few more insults slung at me before I made it to the front barrier. The same lie I used before was enough to quell their anger. The staff at the barrier looked flustered. I didn't need to ask why the ferry wasn't running. They were repeating the same thing over and over: "The engineers need more time; this is for your own safety."

"*When will they be finished?*" a couple of passengers shouted. "*We need to get home.*"

I felt stupid for thinking otherwise, but when I looked past the barrier staff, I saw the crew in a heated discussion. I couldn't hear what they were saying, but maintenance on the ferry wasn't enough to warrant their worried expressions. Or maybe it was – what did I know? I still couldn't shake off the feeling that something was off. I knew I wasn't going to get any further here, so I decided to head to reception.

The queue for reception was just as long as the other one I had pushed through. I had already wasted too much time, and I felt I'd get no more information from here than I would from Penny's radios.

Many scenarios were racing through my mind, making my head pound. If my Kraken had been discovered already, then surely it would have made the news? The reasons for it not making the news would be what? A lack of information. If a lack of information was the reason, then who would listen? And who had the power to keep all vessels docked?

As I walked past the seafront, I noticed that there were no boats at sea, not even small fishing vessels. Judging from the Black Swan's nautical theme earlier, I assumed that the pub would be the place that many seafarers occupied, and so the best place to get information.

***

The atmosphere was completely different to the first time I walked through the Black Swan's door. Now, the pub was busy with excited and animated customers.

The same barman from earlier nodded his head to me in acknowledgement before he served a customer.

I sat at the bar and listened while I waited.

"One minute, they were signalling the distress call, and the next, they were gone," explained one punter.

"*It has something to do with those fucking plesiosaurs. Ships have been sinking others all year to get their dino gold,*" a customer shouted over the others.

"It was a bloody research ship."

"Maybe. Whoever sunk 'em probably didn't know."

"Didn't care, you mean," another answered.

"My daughter told me it was a Kraken." I looked over at the man who said this. He must be Penny's dad.

"Fuck off, John. She's just winding you up," declared the first punter.

Penny's dad laughed it off, then he took a gulp of his pint.

"I'm telling you, it's to do with those plesiosaurs," added the shouter.

"Nah, we haven't had that many ships go down in such a short amount of time," yet another argued.

"What may I get you?" asked the barman.

"It's definitely something to do with the military because it's not on the news," the first punter piped up again.

"Hello. What may I get you?" the barman asked again.

"Huh? Sorry, I was miles away. May I have a Diet Coke, please?" I said.

When he brought me my drink, I asked him if he had seen Penny. He said he hadn't, then he nodded to her dad, John, and told me he hadn't either.

I found a table at the back of the pub and let their voices blend into the background. I had no doubt they were talking about my Kraken. So, it took down a research ship. What was that research ship doing to it? I purposely created a docile Kraken. Well, docile until it was disturbed. Just like the legend, it was powerful enough to destroy large ships. The human race had a choice: either leave it alone or try to kill it. If they chose the latter, then there would be many deaths. Would these deaths be on my conscience? I thought not. *But what if, like my other characters, it has a mind of its own? What if it starts to view all vessels as a threat?* I put that thought to the back of my mind, left the pub and headed back to Penny's.

As I rounded the corner en route to Penny's home, I saw Missy pissing in someone's front garden, over their beautiful, pink pansies.

"Missy, what are you doing, my sweet angel? Come here." My dog-friendly voice trembled.

She ran towards me excitedly with her lead trailing behind her. Penny was too sharp to be this irresponsible. I scooped up Missy and ran the rest of the way back.

"*Varik,*" I shouted as I opened the door. "*Varik.*"

"*In here. The Kraken has made an appearance. Listen to this,*" he shouted from Penny's communications room.

The radios were going wild with broken voices and static. I couldn't concentrate on that right now.

"Missy was outside wandering about. What do you think happened to Penny?" I still had Missy in my arms.

"It took down a research ship," he said proudly.

"I know."

"You do?" He frowned.

"Look, we need to find out what happened to Penny." I took a seat.

"I'll try her phone again." While the phone was to his ear, he said, "It's ringing, but there's no answer."

I racked my mind for answers, but nothing came up. I should have spoken to her dad before I left. I'd have to go back to the Black Swan, but before I did, I asked, "Have you heard from David or Bowen?"

"I spoke to Bowen." He grinned broadly, displaying his serrated teeth, as his smile always did.

My heart sank twice. Firstly, because I wasn't here to speak to Bowen, and secondly, because of what Varik might have said. "What did he say?"

"He blamed me for everything."

"You said you were happy to take the blame."

"I said I was happy for you to blame me, not for him to accuse me," he explained, smirking. "So, I gave him something to think about."

"What?"

"I told him I had located the Kraken, and it was close to his ship."

"Oh, Varik, don't you think he's been through enough?" My heart thumped in my chest when I realised that it could become a possibility. No, I wouldn't – and couldn't – allow my thoughts to walk down that path.

"That being said, he's up and about."

"Good." I slumped back in the chair and closed my eyes.

"When the sun goes down, I'll look for Penny, okay?"

"Okay."

My thoughts returned to her. What could have happened to her? Maybe she had dropped Missy's lead, who then ran off. Had Penny not come back because she was still out there looking for her? I hoped not. I told Varik to message Penny to tell her that Missy had been found and was safe.

***

I was in the kitchen making another coffee when I heard Varik's phone ring from the other room.

"*It's Penny,*" he shouted.

"*Just coming,*" I shouted back.

Varik was shouting aggressively down the phone while I poured the hot water into my cup. I slammed the kettle down and ran down the hall. I knew what she'd done with Missy must have been an accident. He didn't have to shout at her like that.

"You touch a fucking hair on her head, and I will rip you to pieces," he snarled.

"Varik." I tried to take the phone from him.

He pushed me away. "I will track you down— Where is she—? If you touch the Watcher—"

"Varik." Who the fucking hell was he speaking to? Chilled blood pumped through my veins. Varik was right. He was right.

"You have thirty minutes to bring her back—" His lips were peeled back, baring his fangs.

I saw that he was about to smash his phone on the floor, so I grabbed his arm to stop him. "He has her; where?" I cupped his face with my right hand. "Where?"

"I don't know. He won't say until he gets what he wants." Varik pulled me to him and wrapped his arms around me until it hurt.

"What does he want? A confession?"

"It doesn't matter, little Watcher. He won't be getting it."

"Varik, just tell me what Gary wants, and we will give it to him. Penny is more important – you know that." I couldn't imagine what she was going through right now; my mind wouldn't allow it.

"I will track her down tonight and bring her back. He can't have taken her far."

"Tell me what he wanted." Why was he keeping this to himself? "Just tell me."

Varik lifted my hands and squeezed them gently. "He believes that the only way to stop you from writing is to remove your hands."

I laughed at first; Varik's humour could be so dry at times. But this wasn't the time for misplaced humour. I waited for him to smirk or, well, something. Realisation settled in the pit of my stomach when he did neither. I blinked. "What?"

"He wants your hands."

CHAPTER 8

Both my hands were trembling as I looked down at them. I, unlike some, did not take my hands for granted. Talking about hands and their importance was something I had discussed many times over the years with my barber colleagues. I had often watched my hands while I cut hair and wondered how they operated on their own accord. Something that always mystified me was when a client would ask for a haircut I hadn't done before; I might not know how to do that haircut, but my hands always did. All of us barbers marvelled over our hands and the little control we had over them. It was both impressive and creepy. Subconsciously, if you were to fall, your hands automatically stretched out to take the impact, but not for us they didn't. We would rather fall headfirst than risk our livelihoods. I also knew this to be true from my own experience. I rubbed my fingers over the small scar on my forehead.

"What are we going to do?" I asked.

"You're not going to do anything. I will pick up her

scent and track her down." He snaked his hands through the curtains carefully, to minimise light exposure, then he opened a window.

"Are you certain you can find her?"

He raised his brow. "Yes. Then after I do, I will deal with Gary. Agreed?"

I nodded.

Varik's phone rang again. "It's him."

Fury and hatred vibrated through my body. "Let me answer."

Varik rolled his eyes before he passed the phone to me.

"Gary, it's Zoe. You had the audacity to question me in my shop and now you want me to mutilate myself in exchange for a young girl you snatched off the streets. What the fuck do you think you're playing at?"

"You need to be stopped. I have left a gift for you on the driveway. It's time you saw your vampire for what *it* really is. Then, you will have minutes to decide what to do, stay with *it* or leave *it* behind – assuming it can't leave the house during the day, that is."

"What are you doing, Gary? Return Penny now or I will call the police. You will be charged with holding someone against their will." I knew instantly my threat had fallen flat. I could tell he was beyond reasoning with. "How about I confess, then? Would that make you happy?"

"Happy?" He laughed without humour. "Tick tock, Zoe; as I said, you only have minutes left to decide."

The line went dead, and I heard a car outside speed away.

I didn't need to relay the conversation to Varik; he had heard it all. His face was unreadable. He ran his hand through his hair and took a seat. He was calm, and I couldn't work out why.

"What do you think is outside? And why do you think I only have minutes to decide something?" I turned his face to mine.

"He's dug up the body I fed from last night. It's on the driveway. I can scent it from here."

My heart hammered and I started to shake with adrenaline. "We need to leave now. I reckon he's called the police, don't you?"

A body on the driveway would result in us getting arrested on the spot. I ran into the kitchen to hunt for Penny's car keys. There were too many appliances on every surface to see them clearly. Maybe she kept her keys by the door like I did? As I ran to the door, knocking numerous pieces of electrical equipment over, I was crushed at there not being any hooks. It was then that I heard sirens in the distance. "Varik, hurry, help me find her keys."

"No, little Watcher." He stood in the hallway with Missy in his arms. There was tenderness in his eyes, which softened his features. It was a look that was only reserved for Goodboy or for Missy, when he thought I wasn't looking.

"What do you mean 'no'? Varik, if they arrest you, it won't take them long to figure out you're not human. You can't kill them; you know that, don't you?"

The sound of the sirens was closing in, and he just stood there.

"How will you find Penny if you are arrested?" What the hell was he doing? I took Missy from his arms. "Just help me find her keys."

"You can't drive and neither can I during the day."

"Then think of something, for fuck's sake."

"You will take Missy and hide. I will allow myself to get arrested and leave their company without anyone getting hurt, okay? Afterwards, I will find you."

"No, I can't leave you."

"Here, take my phone," he said, then he opened the door. His eyes slammed shut.

"Okay, but—"

"*Go now,*" he bellowed.

I ran and fell through the door; as I was falling, Varik pulled me back up.

His eyes were still shut when he kissed my temple lightly. "Do not look at it," he whispered.

"Varik, please come with us."

"I can't. Go, now."

I was looking back over my shoulder when I tripped again. I turned quickly so Missy wouldn't take the impact. I landed with my back bent over something – it was the body.

The man's eyes were wide open, like those of a rabbit caught in the headlights. His mouth looked as though he had died screaming. Dried blood was splattered over his face, and his grey jumper was drenched with it. But that's not what shocked me the most – no, that was the man's throat; it had been ripped out. His head was only attached by what I believed was his spine. Bile rose in my throat, and my skin pricked hot and cold.

This was what Gary wanted me to see. He wanted me to be horrified by this, and I was. He wanted me to turn my back on Varik, and I suppose any other person would, or would they?

I scrambled to my feet and set Missy down. She wanted to investigate the body, which made me retch. "Come on, girl."

A police car screeched past as I turned off the drive and headed around the corner. I didn't even look in their direction. With no destination in mind, I headed straight to the harbour. I had no choice but to wait for Varik.

As I turned towards the town, I ran down a side alley and sprayed vomit all over the wall and floor. Afterwards, I sat with my head between my knees for a while to catch my breath. When I eventually made my way back onto the main street, I saw another police car speed past. Images of Varik being arrested ran through my mind. *Please don't resist arrest, Varik,* I thought.

A car pulled up to the side of me. I already knew who it was, and I carried on walking.

"*You made the right choice, Zoe, leaving that leech behind,*" Gary shouted through his open window.

"His name is Varik, and he is not a leech. That man you dumped on the driveway was, though."

"So, even after you've seen his handiwork, you still side with him." Gary looked smug. Was he enjoying his sick game? I chose not to answer him; I owed him nothing. "That test, by the way, was your last chance. Clearly, you are just as evil as your creations."

Evil?

I came to an abrupt stop and stuck my head through his window. I took pleasure in the fact that he cowered. Then I pulled his keys out of the ignition and put them in my back pocket. "You don't know what evil is. If you knew how Varik chose his prey, then you would. There are a lot of sick people in this world, and that prick you dumped on the driveway was one of them."

He was about to speak when I wrapped my hands around his neck. I used my telekinesis to force his body towards me, holding him in place. His eyes were wide with terror. A part of me that I never knew existed revelled in it. I wanted him to fear me.

"See that pub behind me? Penny's dad is inside. How about we walk over there and you explain to him why you took his daughter, then we will call the police so you can explain to them why there is DNA in the boot of your car from a convicted sex offender. Assuming that was how you transported *it*." I hissed the word '*it*' like he had done when he spoke of Varik.

His eyes widened even more before he tried to speak. I loosened my grip to allow him to. "I will not give you her location without your hands. That's the deal."

I shoved him back before I let go. The cars behind him started to beep their horns. "You have taken an innocent girl, Gary."

"Is she? She stupidly defended *it* and begged for *its* life. Someone needs to stop you, and if this is the only way, then so be it."

"You are a self-righteous prick. What you're doing is far worse than what I did to you. I wasn't aware at the time, but you are. If anyone needs to be stopped, it's you," I snapped, then I sighed, "and you will be."

"Zoe, if you don't give me what I want, then she will die. Although, I suppose she's as bad as you. Perhaps it will be a win-win situation if you don't make the right decision."

His arrogance returned, igniting my temper. I could feel my whole body thrumming with energy, getting ready to crush every bone in his body. A memory of Penny clinking her beer bottle with mine the night before made me see sense. Varik was certain he could track her down, but what if he couldn't? I had to keep my options open.

Gary and I wouldn't be coming to an agreement on this; neither of us would be swayed. I had no choice but to walk away.

"*My keys,*" Gary shouted.

I turned and pushed out my palm towards his car, which I slammed to the other side of the road using my telekinesis.

A car coming from the opposite direction crashed into his bonnet. Car horns erupted all down the road. I glanced back at Gary, who looked bewildered – good. There was more where that came from.

***

A few hours had passed since I left Penny's home. I found myself sitting on the same bench I had sat on earlier that day. I kept my eyes on the people sitting on the bench next to mine. They were eating fish and chips. I knew, judging from the size of their portion, that they wouldn't be eating it all. I remembered a time when I couldn't afford such a luxury; not to buy more food than I needed, but buying food in general. Being left without a guardian at eighteen and having to fend for myself had been a gruelling challenge. People often say it's eat or heat, without really knowing the full meaning of it. I, however, did know. If it were not for David, I most certainly would have gone to bed with an empty stomach on many occasions.

The couple wrapped up their chips and half-eaten fish and were about to throw it in the bin as they walked past.

"I'll take that." I got off the bench and walked over to them.

"Excuse me." The man smirked.

The woman he was with hid her smile behind her hands. He just stood there gaping at me, so I unwrapped the paper while it was still in his hands and took out the battered fish. As I turned to leave I heard them laugh.

"Dirty beggar; I haven't seen one do that before," she said.

I ignored them, picked up Missy, then sat back down on the bench with her on my lap. She scoffed down the fish in seconds and licked all the oil from my fingers. "Good girl." The money I had borrowed from Penny had run out earlier that day, and although I was okay with going without food tonight, I couldn't bear it if Missy did. I wanted to be angry at Varik again, for leaving all my belongings in David's car, but that mattered very little now.

I was tempted to call Goodboy to me for extra company. I had never felt so lonely as I did right now. But the thought of him being by Bowen's side changed my mind. Maybe David would check in with me at Penny's soon, and realise I wasn't there? A single tear slid down my cheek at the thought of him going there only to find the place swarming with police. We'd all been through so much in such a short amount of time.

My heart rate slowly started to come back down while I watched the day turn to night. "Varik won't be long now," I sang to Missy.

***

It was almost midnight, and both Missy and I were still sitting on the bench, shivering. My thoughts turned to Penny again; I hoped Gary had the sense to not keep her out in the open. She must be so frightened. If I really had to choose between my hands and her life, of course it would be her. I smiled, but only briefly. Was Gary expecting me to cut off my own hands? I wondered if he had even thought that through. Perhaps it was a part of his plan to do it himself. Could he really do that to me? Maybe. He was a broken man now. More tears formed in my eyes.

I looked at the time again: two minutes past midnight. Where was he? So many horrible scenarios whipped through my mind. What if Varik couldn't get away. What if they hurt him, and he felt like he had no choice but to retaliate? One thought did rear its ugly head, but no, Varik would not abandon us.

Not knowing what to do and realising I couldn't stay out in the open for much longer, I headed towards Penny's dad's boat.

I walked down the stone jetty to his boat and looked up towards the Black Swan. A few people were still inside, but no one was walking along the streets. Perhaps the circus outside Penny's house was keeping everyone occupied. Her poor father must be going out of his mind with worry. Although he wasn't a conventional father, from what Penny had told me, they were extremely close.

I unravelled the cords holding down the tarp and put Missy through first before I slipped in. I used the torch on my phone to look around. What would there be on a seal-watching boat? Nothing. Wait, there were thin cushion pads on the seats. I pulled them all off and put them on the wooden floor. I lay on my side and let Missy curl up into me.

My head was pounding; for the first time in a long time, I willed my body to sleep. I breathed in for five seconds, held it for five more, then released it.

***

I was dreaming about Bowen running his hand through my hair, only for it to continue after I woke. "Varik?"

"Little Watcher."

I sat up, hitting my head on the tarp above. I used the light from my phone to see him. He sat cross-legged behind me. He hissed at me when I shone the light in his face to look for any injuries. He had none.

"Are you okay? What happened?" I swept his fringe from his eyes.

"I was cuffed in the back of the police car on the driveway. When the sun went down, I broke the cuffs and kicked open the door. No one got hurt." I could tell he added that last bit just to keep me from worrying.

"We need to find Penny."

"She's with her father."

"What?"

He smirked at me, laced his fingers behind his head and leaned back, like the arrogant shit I knew and loved. Then he reached into his pocket and dangled keys in my face. I slapped them away.

"Varik, answer me. What happened?"

"She was tied to a tree in the woods, about two mile away."

"That vile bastard tied her to a tree? It's freezing out. Is she okay?"

"She seemed okay to me. She wants Gary dead." He dangled the keys closer to my face.

I slapped them away again. "What did he say to her? How did he get her?"

"What does it matter? His car has been seized—"

"Yeah, I pushed it across the road, and another car smashed into it."

"You did? Impressive. And Penny has given a statement to the police. Gary can't get far now. We will deal with him when we get back." He rattled the keys right in my face this time, so I knocked his arm away.

"Get back from where? We have nowhere to go."

"There are people looking for me. I can't hide in here all day." He held up the keys. "Penny gave me these, and they just so happen to be for this boat."

We both grinned.

"Where will we go?" I questioned, but I already knew. I checked the time. The *AmberIvy* was roughly six hours away. My heart sank instantly. "We won't make it in time."

"We will if we meet them in the middle."

***

Varik was much better at driving the small boat than the car. That being said, there were no other boats to crash into out here.

After we unwrapped the tarp and fired up the engine, a few people from the pub ran out to stop us. Varik waved them goodbye while I hid behind my hands. We didn't know where we were going. Varik assured me that if the *AmberIvy* were heading down from the Faroe Islands, we would head towards it. I only hoped that we would soon get their coordinates or they would get ours.

"*Can you see that wooden box over there?*" he shouted over the engine's roar and the wind.

"Yeah."

"I smell water in it. You need to drink."

What I thought was a bench for the seal-watching tourists had a lock on it. I walked back over to Varik, holding on to the rails as I did, then rifled through the bunch of keys, looking for a small silver one.

"There isn't a key on here that matches the lock."

"Take the wheel. Do not steer it left or right. Just keep it steady."

I gripped the wheel tightly and looked over at all the equipment. The radio was on, but only static came through. Varik had already tried to contact the *AmberIvy*, but we couldn't get a clear line. I did hear Captain Harry's voice briefly, but I don't think he heard us. The coastguard, however, could be heard, loud and clear. They demanded that we turn around. They were more concerned for our safety than the fact that we had just stolen a boat. Still, it was one less thing to worry about when they made no attempt to follow us.

I heard the wooden box splinter when Varik kicked the lid off. Missy whined, and my heart warmed when I heard him apologise to her. I looked around and watched him pour water into his cupped hand for her to drink from.

"Eyes forwards, Watcher."

"Oh, yeah. Was there anything else in the box?" My stomach rumbled in the hope that there could be food in there.

"Just water and whisky." He took the wheel back, then handed me a bottle.

"Thank you. What does the boat keep hitting?" I asked just as we hit something big enough to jolt us back.

"Debris from other boats and ships. A lot of ships have been destroyed fighting over the plesiosaurs. You can't see it because it's dark, but it's all around us. There's a lot more than the last time I was at sea, and it's going to get worse the further out we go."

"Do you think the Kraken was responsible for some of this too?" It was funny how I had completely forgotten about that until now. Hopefully, our small boat wouldn't be perceived as a threat.

He smirked. "Maybe. Does it upset you?"

Oddly, it didn't. Obviously, I was scared for the *AmberIvy* and *Ocean Warriors*, but if the Kraken made people think twice about hunting my plesiosaurs, then so be it. At that point, Penny's dad came to mind, betraying my initial thoughts. "I'm ashamed to say."

"That's just the human part of you. Listen, other than David, Bowen, the dogs and the crew, the rest don't matter. It's just us. I keep telling you that."

I stood behind him and wrapped my arms around his waist. I didn't know what to say. Our family came first, of course, but shouldn't you feel compassion for all people? I had to admit to myself that I didn't. I couldn't. Why should I? Yet, at the same time, I felt guilty for feeling that way.

Wanting to change the subject, I asked Varik how much longer we had to go.

"It's hard to say. A couple more hours. Try calling the *AmberIvy*'s phone, and I'll try the radio again."

I did and got nothing. I kept my eyes on what I thought was the horizon, relieved that there wasn't a sliver of light. If the sun came up before we made contact, I didn't think I could drive this boat.

"Varik, come in. Over." Captain Harry's voice sounded distorted, but it was loud and clear.

"What are your coordinates? Over."

While Varik spoke to Harry, I collapsed onto one of the seats. The relief I felt was like no other. I was hours away from being with Bowen. Soon, we would all be home.

"Poppet."

Relief rushed through me. I looked up to see David standing over me. I jumped up to wrap my arms around him.

His face was like thunder. "What are you doing here? I told you to stay at Penny's."

I tried to tell him everything over the roaring engine. At first, he kept looking at Varik accusingly, but as the story unfolded, he went from looking bewildered to furious. He then bollocked me for not telling him about Gary sooner. I explained to him that neither Varik nor I knew it would escalate to this.

"Will the police be looking for you, too?" he queried.

"I'm not sure. Probably. It will depend on what Penny tells them." I was sure they would be. The complaint Gary made against me before we left for Oban and the fact that we were both here at the same time would raise a lot of questions. I didn't want to think about that right now. Penny was safe, and at that moment, so was Bowen.

"I strongly suggest we keep our heads down for a very long time when we return to Witney," David said.

"Agreed."

We both smiled at each other.

"Come here." He pulled me in for a tight cuddle, then he walked up a couple of steps to where Varik was.

The sea was getting choppier, and I had to hold tightly to the railing.

"Thank you for looking out for her." David clapped him on the back.

"She can look out for herself. Did she tell you she slammed Gary's car across the road?" Varik asked.

David gave me an if-looks-could-kill stare, then he shook his head. "No, she didn't."

"How's Bowen?" I asked, wanting both to know and to change the subject.

"He's fine for now. When Captain Harry relays your coordinates to the *Ocean Warriors*, he won't be."

"Any Kraken sightings?" I asked to change the subject again.

"Yeah, there have been now. It took down a fleet of poachers east of Scotland. The remaining ship lost power and lived to tell the tale. We've come to the conclusion that the Kraken doesn't respond kindly to engine noise."

"Shit."

"Is that all you have to say? The *AmberIvy* and *Ocean*

Warriors are sailing back half-a-mile apart to keep the noise levels low."

"Which ship will we be boarding? I want to see Bowen as soon as possible."

"The *Ocean Warriors* is in front. We'll drop you off there, then Varik and I will continue."

"No David," Varik said. "We'll pick Bowen up. I wanted to play a game we used to play with Goodboy. I would stand port side and Bowen to starboard, then we would both call out to Goodboy, to see who he loved the most."

I had heard about them playing that game. David rolled his eyes.

"This time," Varik continued. "The Watcher and I will play. We will stick Bowen in the middle and see who he chooses."

CHAPTER 9

David's arrival couldn't have come at a better time: the sun was coming up. We found a hat within one of the boxes, with a seal-watching-tour logo on it, perhaps belonging to Penny's dad. Varik wore it, pulling it down low to protect his eyes in case he opened them accidently. David found life jackets inside another bench storage box before he took over from Varik. Both Varik and I wore one. I helped him get into his, then he tied us to the railing with a thin, corded rope. This small boat was not designed for the powerful waves and was starting to fill up with seawater. Every time debris and waves hit us side on, the boat threatened to capsize. Varik assured me that he could break our restraints if it did. As we rocked from side to side, Missy yelped and trembled in my arms; I couldn't console her.

I called over to David to see how much further we had to go, but I didn't think he heard me. My eyes stung. Saltwater was continuously being splashed into my face, and I could no longer see clearly. The rope used to tie me down was starting to cut into my waist more frequently. When a wave came over the boat, smashing itself against my back, my head was thrown forwards. Pain shot up and down my neck.

"*Brace yourself,*" Varik bellowed in my ear.

"*What?*"

We hit something in the water – hard. The rope wrapped around my waist snapped, propelling me to the other side of the boat. I heard a sharp pop when Missy's small head hit the railing. Through my hazy, salt-filled eyes, I could see blood gushing over her little brown-and-white body. Her skull had been cracked wide open.

"*No. No.*" Her body was floppy in my arms. "*Missy, no!*"

Varik grabbed me from behind just as something else hit our boat. I couldn't keep my grip on Missy, and I couldn't open my eyes to find her when another wave struck me in the face.

"*She's gone,*" Varik shouted over the roar of the wind, waves and engine.

"*Where is she?*" I screamed.

"*The waves took her.*"

Varik tightened his grip on me, then retied us to the railing with the remaining rope. One moment, I was looking at Missy's blood through my bleary eyes, but the next, another wave had washed it away. It was as if she never existed. I screamed until my throat burned. *How could I let this happen? Why are we out here?* I was desperately trying to write a story in my head for Missy. *I will not lose her like this.* I felt another loud bang, this one vibrated throughout the whole boat and was louder than the others before it. "What was that?"

"David can't avoid the debris. The waves are crashing it into us."

I was on my knees, holding on to rope attached to the railing; the cold water surrounding my waist froze me to my bones. I felt stiff and knew I wouldn't be able to move if I had to. Another loud bang made me jump. "Is that smoke I can smell?"

"The engine has packed up," Varik explained.

"We're not going to make it, are we?"

"Yes, we are, little Watcher. Yes, we are." He tightened his arms around me.

I managed to open my eyes in time to see David aim a flare gun upwards, then fire it. For a brief moment, I thought he looked out of place. A year ago, he was just a bookseller, and I was just a barber. How both our lives had changed so dramatically in that time! Yet, it was as if, somehow, it had escaped my notice.

I looked over the side of the boat and saw nothing but grey waves and shipwreck debris. I called over to David, wanting to know if he could see anything from his side. He still couldn't hear me, and even if he had done, I couldn't hear him.

In the distance, I heard a horn blare for a few seconds. I could still hear the horns echoing after it stopped. "What was that, Varik? Was it a ship?"

"It's a ship."

David shot another flare into the sky. He turned to say something, but as he did, the horn blared again from the oncoming ship. Did it sound closer this time?

"*What did he say?*" I shouted to Varik.

"It's the *Ocean Warriors.*"

Relief swept through me, only for it to be diminished seconds later. I felt cheated. It was only minutes ago that Missy lost her life – and because of me. I needed to be with Bowen now, more than ever. Only he could take this pain away.

David waded through the water to us. He started to unravel the rope that secured us to the railing.

I looked down at the knot he was trying to undo. "What are you doing?"

"We're going down. I'm going to tie you to Varik."

"What about you?" Another wave struck me in my face.

"I will be fine, poppet. The dead can't die again, can they?" I could tell from his tone that he was trying to lighten the situation. Something was wrong.

When my eyes cleared momentarily, he looked shell-shocked. Realisation hit me when he cupped my head in his hands and his eyes darted all over my face, as if he were memorising it. He didn't think I was going to make it. I wasn't going to make it.

He then grabbed Varik roughly and kissed him on the head. "Do not let her go. I will deploy a small boat from the *Ocean Warriors*. I will be back for you both."

"I won't. Okay. Hurry," Varik replied.

I looked over my shoulder to see Varik with his eyes tightly closed while he nodded in David's direction.

I looked over the railing again, but I still couldn't see the *Ocean Warriors*. The side of the boat dipped into the ocean while more water gushed in.

"Poppet, you need to get off the boat now and start swimming. Do not look back."

Varik stood up behind me, bringing me up with him. I was about to lift my foot over the side of the boat, when it dipped down and disappeared for the last time. I looked forwards and swam with everything I had.

***

As I gasped for breath, I inhaled seawater. My eyes stung, and I felt disorientated. Varik shouted something, but I couldn't hear the words. When something struck my head, I screamed, then choked on more water. My legs no longer had the strength to kick out. All I could do was grab on to Varik's shoulder with one hand. A wave rolled over us, sending us under.

The roar of the elements was muted instantly. It was calm down here; peaceful. All the tension in my body evaporated after I accepted the inevitable. When Varik tightened his grip on me, I burned it into my memory. My last memory.

***

The pain in my chest was like no other. I tried to move my arms and open my eyes; however, I could do neither. My ears were ringing, but I could still hear faint voices beyond it. Was that Bowen's voice? It was. I concentrated on his voice like it was a lifeline, and I fought against my own body's restraints.

"Don't move, sweetheart; don't move." He brushed his hand over my temple to my jaw.

The sound of his voice and his touch gave me the strength to break through my paralysis. My eyes shot open. Disappointment flashed through my heart momentarily when I saw my eyes staring back at me, but not for long – it was always his devastating smile that gave life to his eyes.

A hoarse hissing sound left my lips when I tried to say his name.

"Don't speak, baby. You're okay now." He made no attempt to wipe away the tears that streamed down his cheek. "We almost lost you."

I moved my arm up to touch him, but it wouldn't

cooperate. Frustration overrode my joy, followed by dread. I could feel my lungs tightening. "Va …"

"Varik?"

I dipped my head down once in an attempt to nod.

He stepped back and gently moved my head to the side. Varik was lying in a bed next to mine. He had fresh bandages wrapped around his head, to cover his eyes, and another bandage was wrapped around his torso. There was a tube running from his wrist to a blood bag that was hooked above his bed. I tried to point in its direction. What had happened to him?

As if reading my mind, Bowen answered, "We had to remove a large, twisted piece of metal from his side. He lost a lot of blood, which has already been replaced. That bag above his head is to keep him nourished."

I looked back to Bowen and finally found the strength to lift my hand to his face. He looked so pale. "Your … bloo …"

"Yeah, my blood." He took my hand from his face and kissed it, then straightened my engagement ring.

"Goodboy, Da … David …"

"David is here. He wanted to give us time alone together. Goodboy is sleeping on the other side of Varik's bed." He smiled, although his eyes were still wet with tears.

I tried to speak again, but this time I really concentrated on my words. What I needed to say next was important: "I love you."

"I love you too," he whispered, then he put his knee onto the bed to lift himself up. He laid his body against mine and pulled me to him.

I breathed in his unique scent, remembering a time when I thought I would never experience it again. His hot tears fell freely from his eyes onto my neck.

"Oh Zoe, when I saw you both floating … I thought you were both dead. I thought you were gone."

"Sorry, Bowen," I rasped, not knowing what else to say.

"We lowered one of the small boats in preparation when we saw the flares. Then David came and told us to get in it; we did and we headed towards you both. If we hadn't, we wouldn't have got to you in time."

When Bowen cried, I cried with him.

I stroked his hair back from his face, then ran my hand down the stubble on his cheek. My voice hitched when I tried to talk. So I just did what I could: I used all my strength to hold him.

**

The captain of the *Ocean Warriors* had dropped anchor shortly after Varik and I were rescued. That was two days ago. The *AmberIvy* had also anchored nearby. We boarded it just a few hours ago, using one of its small boats.

The *Ocean Warriors'* crew were uneasy at having a vampire on board, which I totally understood. Although, if you were to ask me, they seemed more uneasy with my presence than his. Bowen explained to me that after they pulled him, Oscar and Lana out of the water, they commented on their identical eye colour. Officer Blake – whose first name is Nathan, or Nate for short – wouldn't stop interrogating Bowen until he came clean. Blake also had his suspicions surrounding the disappearance and reappearance of the *AmberIvy*, and had also witnessed the Kraken's destructive nature from afar, along with other crew members. With all that and the impossible existence of the plesiosaurs, he demanded answers. Bowen told him everything from start to finish, knowing that there was very little Blake could do with the truth anyway. Still, they were kind enough to allow me and Varik to get our strength back before our departure.

I was lying back on the bottom bunk in Bowen's cabin when he opened his door and entered.

"What are you smiling at?" he said, then he moved me over so he could stretch out beside me.

"Because you're back, and I was thinking about the difference between the two crews. The *Ocean Warriors'* crew couldn't get us off fast enough, but our crew couldn't have made us feel more welcome if they tried."

We were applauded when we arrived. I had never been applauded before in my life. The crew thanked me for their lives. Lana, who died with Bowen, gave me the longest hug, followed by her boyfriend, Rory, who was first mate to Captain Harry. He was actually one of my creations, as were the second and third mate. Some of the crew weren't. It was about time I had faces to go with the names Bowen had spoken so fondly of.

"True, the *Ocean Warriors'* crew were … wary—"

"Scared."

"Yeah, or scared. But they are still our allies."

"I know, and I'm thankful for that. Did you manage to speak to your mum?" While I was in the shower, Bowen had left to phone his mum. It was the first time we'd been out of each other's sight since we'd been reunited.

"I did. She's worried, but I explained everything to her."

Well, not everything, I hoped. The Kraken had finally made the news, but not as we expected. All seafarers were being called back on the grounds of war at sea. That, I already knew from the discussions I'd heard in the Black Swan. Ships wanting to capture the plesiosaurs weren't just blowing up their defenders, they were also taking out the competition, with an unprecedented urgency. The news was only partially true. Without actual video footage and only the sworn statements of bewildered crew members from illegal ships, there was not enough evidence to broadcast the full story. This surprised me, given how our so-called 'free-state news broadcasters' operated these days.

"How much longer will we be at sea?" I enquired.

"Every thirty minutes, we will start the engines and sail for approximately thirty minutes. We will alternate between the two ships. That's if we don't detect the Kraken through radar. If that happens, we'll kill the engines." He spoke without worry, which gave me confidence.

"I can't wait to get back home and leave all this behind us."

"What, you don't like my cabin?" He grinned, then sobered. "Sweetheart, we won't be able to leave all this behind us anytime soon. We need to deal with Gary, and we need to make a decision about the Kraken."

Bowen had slammed his fist down on to a table when we first told him about what Gary had done and what he wanted from me. Varik said he wanted Gary dead; no one, not even David, disagreed. I, however, still felt uneasy about it. I couldn't let go of the fact that this was my doing. A small part of me still wanted to make things right with him, even after what he had done to Penny. But I knew now that I didn't have much of a choice.

"Varik will deal with Gary," I said quietly. "As for my Kraken, you mean whether we should kill it or not?"

"Maybe you can write a story about how it died?" His eyes softened.

"I have no control over my creations once they're out, you know that."

"I know. You could write a story about a ship taking it down."

I studied the eyes in his face – mine in place of his pale-brown ones. They were becoming his, as if he had been born with them. However, hearing him talk about the death of my Kraken brought a pang to my chest. My mind drifted to the scene in my head of it lying across the sea mound it once called home, with its tentacles swaying lazily with the current as it slept peacefully. The thought of it dying needlessly seemed extreme.

"It's harmless, Bowen."

He smirked at me and shook his head. "Is it? We don't need to discuss it right now anyway, but think about what the world would be like if we couldn't use the ocean again."

"No more around-the-world cruises." My sarcastic tone was laced with bitterness.

"Ah, I see Varik has rubbed off on you while I have been away."

"Away? Dead you mean. Did you die because I created the plesiosaurs or because of human greed?"

"Human greed," he said simply. "Listen, sweetheart, there are many innocent seafarers. Take Penny's dad, for example."

I already had. "You're right, we don't need to talk about this right now." I ran my hand down his chest.

He shook his head before his mischievous eyes lit up. He sat up and pulled his jumper off over his head while I unzipped his jeans. Then, he stopped my hand. "Are you still in pain? Any at all?"

"No, I'm fine." I wasn't, as my chest still felt heavy and my head still pounded, but I needed to feel him.

I took my t-shirt off, thankful that it was the only thing I was wearing, while he kicked off his jeans. I brought my knees up and opened my legs for him, knowing he liked this, and I watched as he kneeled in front of me. He was already hard, but I knew he'd still take his time with me before he gave me what I really wanted.

"Come here." I pulled his head to mine.

I felt his broad tip for only a second before he trailed his tongue down my neck to my breasts. I shuffled down lower, desperate for him to be inside me, then I groaned in frustration right before he moved his hand between my legs. He groaned while he kissed my breasts.

"Bowen, now," I said urgently.

He didn't listen, instead his fingers moved faster, until my every muscle begged for release. My toes curled when I moaned, and my body exploded with pure bliss. Finally, Bowen pushed my knee to my shoulder, then eased into me. His rhythm was steady at first, then quickened towards the end. I ran my hands over his shoulders and down his back, and I knew, without a doubt, that no other man on this planet could make me feel like he does. When he came, I joined him.

"I've missed you, Zoe," he panted.

"And I've missed you."

"Remind me not to leave you again."

We turned to face each other.

"Oh, I will."

***

Someone was running up and down the passageway, shouting and banging on all the doors. "Come quickly," they called out. "Come now."

I glanced at Bowen, but he looked as confused as I felt. Then he nodded his head as if he remembered something, and he told me that it couldn't be an emergency, which meant it could only be one other thing.

"What is it?" I asked while he quickly got dressed.

"You'll see."

He pulled a jumper from his chest by the foot of the bunk and shoved it over my head. I laughed and asked again what it was. Maybe this was how they announced that the food was ready. My stomach rumbled.

"You'll see; come on, quickly."

We ran through the door and down the narrow passageway.

"Little Watcher."

I spun around and saw Varik jogging up behind us. "What's going on?" I asked him.

"Don't tell her; it's a surprise." Bowen was tugging me away.

I couldn't stop giggling. What could be so exciting?

Varik grinned, then he handed Bowen his phone. "It's day; will you film them for me?"

Film them? Oh wow, am I finally about to see my beautiful plesiosaurs? I hoped so.

"Yes, Varik, I will film the whales," he said mechanically, then he took the phone from Varik.

As soon as Bowen opened the hatch to the top deck, he stood behind me and covered my eyes with his hands.

"This way," he said. "A couple more steps. Hold your hand until …"

I grabbed hold of the railing.

"That's it."

I could hear the crew oohing and ahhing. I tried to move Bowen's hands out of the way, but they wouldn't budge.

"Not yet. There was something I wanted to tell you," he stated.

"Okay." I giggled again.

"I never wanted you to stop writing your stories – ever. I just wanted to protect you, that's all, and to be a part of the decisions you were making, so you didn't find yourself in a situation that could have been avoided. And I do love all your characters, including the questionable ones, because they are all a part of you. Do you understand?"

I nodded the best I could while his hands were still over my eyes.

"Because without your stories, we wouldn't have these." He took his hands away.

At first I couldn't see anything because my eyes hadn't adjusted, but when they did: "Bowen, look at them!"

There seemed to be a family of four; no, five. No, there were six. They swam with all the elegance of a seal underwater. When they rolled near the surface of the water, exposing their stomachs, their four flippers glided smoothly back under, hardly leaving a ripple behind. I gripped the railing harder, so I could have a closer look. Their mottled, grey-brown skin glistened in the sun. "Look at their beautiful faces. Bowen, look at their eyes." I pointed.

"I know. Can you see those dolphins over there? They're called white-beaked common dolphins. We always see them together."

"You do? Of course, I remember you telling me, but why?" I had seen them many times on the news, not that you could ever compare that to what I was seeing right then, but I hadn't seen them with dolphins before.

"Our guess is that both species have come to the conclusion that there is safety in numbers. Or maybe they just like each other's company? Who knows."

"Hey, that one doesn't have my eyes; they look dark

brown, or maybe black." How strange. What could be the reason for that?

"It's a new discovery; I wanted to share it with you when I got back. That one there" – he pointed – "is not one of your creations. We knew they were breeding, but we hadn't seen any offspring yet. That beauty is called Tilikum. One of our crew wanted to name her after a famous whale."

"Her?"

"Yeah, if you remember from your story, you gave the males a dark crest between the eyes."

"I remember." I sniffed back tears.

The plesiosaurs were swimming past the ship now. I kept my eyes on Tilikum until she was out of sight. I could have watched them for hours. I thought back to this sickening video going around on social media. It was about a marine park charging, once converted to pounds sterling, around one thousand pounds for a one-hour viewing. The plesiosaur in the tank was motionless; it just floated on the surface, it's flippers, head and tail spread out like the tentacles of a starfish. It had also looked soulless and ready for a death that wouldn't be coming soon enough. The stadium, if you could call it that, was as packed as the London Underground. Children were waving stuffed plesiosaur toys around, and parents were fighting to get a closer look. The noise level was deafening; I remembered having to turn the volume down on my phone. I had wondered why the people there couldn't see it for what it really was: cruelty. Luckily, the majority of the comments below the video clip were of the same opinion as me. Shame on the park and shame on the twats who purchased the tickets was what the comments had mainly said. If the world had come together, they could have been doing plesiosaur-watching tours instead, like what Penny's dad does for a living but with plesiosaurs instead of seals.

How lovely it would have been for the tourists to be out in the open or lucky enough to spot other marine wildlife while out on the tour.

Another hideous reminder of human destruction was the never-ending sea of ship debris. How disgusting it was that my plesiosaurs had to swim through that crap.

"Oh shit. I forgot to film them for Varik," Bowen said, pulling me from my thoughts. He turned to face Rory. "Did you film them?"

Rory nodded. "I did. How incredible was that?"

"Incredible. Will you send that video to Varik?"

"Will do," he said, then he walked off, but not before he gave me a nod and a knowing smile.

I smiled back.

"So, what do you think?" Bowen enquired, which he followed with a kiss.

"Words can't describe … They are perfect."

"As are you. Now, Captain Harry wants a crew meeting today at four o'clock this afternoon. Shall we go down now? Maybe we could get you some food while we wait."

"Yes, I am starving." I took one last look over my shoulder in the hope of seeing my plesiosaurs again, but they had gone. So had any doubt I had regarding my latest creation. Humans would now have to accept that they no longer owned the seven seas. The Kraken would.

***

Something didn't feel right about the canteen, or the passageways, come to think of it. "This wasn't how I designed the *AmberIvy*," I said to myself. I noticed a few of the crew members frowning at me, then they looked around the room trying to figure out what I had meant.

"Yeah, it was. Do you mean since you resurrected her?" Bowen frowned and started to look around. "It looks the same to me."

"This isn't what was in my head when I described this ship in my story."

Bowen looked at me as if he were trying to read my thoughts. "You mean the decor, don't you? Some of the crew live aboard this ship full time. Captain Harry gave them the go-ahead to decorate it how they wanted."

"Ah."

The canteen was now for both food and entertainment. There was a TV in the corner next to a bookcase filled with DVDs and Xbox games. A few of the tables and chairs had been taken out to accommodate a corner sofa. The walls had been painted pale green, but someone had artistically painted what looked like a forest on it.

"The trees help them forget that they are at sea twenty-four-seven," he explained.

"I like it." I faced Bowen, slid my hands across the table to hold his and asked him, "Where's the food?"

"I'll bring you something." He kissed my hand, grinning at the same time.

While I watched him walk away, David came in, followed by Varik and Goodboy. This wouldn't be the first time we'd all been in the same room as each other. No, that was on the *Ocean Warriors* when Varik had finally woken up.

His first words were asking about my well-being. I was able to tell him myself that I was safe and well. He relaxed instantly, then told me and anyone else who would listen that it was because *he* had saved my life. I hugged and thanked him anyway, even though Bowen had told me we were both found unconscious.

"Poppet, I was told you finally got to see your plesiosaurs. Beautiful aren't they?" asked David.

"Yeah, they really are. Are you both okay?" I enquired.

David had been really quiet for the last two days. He said he should have spent more time with Missy. I understood his sorrow; we all have these regrets after a loved one passes. I promised him I'd bring her back as soon as I could get to my laptop. He wanted her back like Goodboy so he wouldn't have to leave her behind again.

"We are," he confirmed. "We're about to pull up the anchor and start a snail's pace sail back to port. Captain Harry wants to do a safety meeting beforehand."

"In other words: how to get the fuck off this ship if the Kraken comes for us." Varik laughed without humour.

"Are there enough small boats?" I wondered. There should be, as I had created this ship that way, but after all the other modifications, I had to ask.

"Yeah, there are. Our main concern is getting all the crew into them in time. Captain Harry will want everyone on deck when we sail, so we'll have a better chance," explained David.

"Sounds right," Varik conceded.

Bowen walked back over with a tray, put it on the table and slid it towards me. "Tomato soup from a tin, how you like it, and pineapple from a tin, also how you like it."

Perfection. "Thank you."

"Before Captain Harry arrives, we need to discuss how we're going to destroy the Kraken," David stated.

Bowen nodded his head in agreement.

"We do?" I blew across the piping-hot tomato soup before putting a spoonful in my mouth.

They both looked at me as if to say, "Yeah, obviously." Varik looked at them both and started laughing while he shook his head.

I stirred my soup slowly, contemplating. After what I had seen today, I knew I wouldn't be doing that. I understood that I may, one day, come to regret my decision. Even so, the death of the Kraken would weigh much heavier on my heart than the threat it posed. Plus, there was another reason: "We can't protect the plesiosaurs, the Kraken can."

I didn't even bother to look up. This soup was really nice.

CHAPTER 10

After the safety meeting, we all stood next to our designated boats and waited for Captain Harry to restart the engines. I was also grateful for the fresh air. David had wanted to discuss the Kraken, and my decision on whether to do anything about it, before our meeting started. But he didn't stop, even when it began. I kept on shushing him and pretended to listen to the captain. The meeting then focused on the Kraken. It was, after all, one of the reasons why we were in our predicament. I kept my eyes focused on nothing in particular every time the crew looked over at me. I had felt relieved when the meeting ended, and I couldn't get out of the canteen fast enough.

The low hum of the engine softly brought the *AmberIvy* to life, and if we were moving forwards, you wouldn't have known it. Each small boat could seat eight passengers, and we had more than enough for our crew, but not every crew member was a small boat pilot. David, Bowen and Varik were. With Varik being unable to do this due to the daylight, the ship was one down. David stood next to a boat on the port side (my boat was on the starboard side). At least he couldn't bollock me from the other side of the ship. Still, the thought of us being separated filled me with dread. I would rather suffer his frustration towards me than this. I gripped Bowen's hand tightly.

"Are you okay, sweetheart?" He squeezed my hand back.

"Yeah, I just wanted us all in the same boat … if the worst happens. We should be fine though, right?" I very much doubted the Kraken would detect us moving at this bloody pace.

"It's just a precaution. We'll be fine. Have you thought about what you're going to do with …?"

Varik leaned forwards in Bowen's direction. "Have you thought about what you're going to say to your mum, Bowen? How will you explain to her that you no longer have the eyes you were born with?"

I smirked at Varik's wide grin. You couldn't focus on much else when the top half of his face was wrapped in a bandana.

"You're a dick, do you know that?" Bowen smirked back. "Varik, what's your opinion on the Kraken?"

"I don't have one. I am looking forward to seeing it, though."

"Well, you seemed to find it quite funny when Zoe said she wouldn't be doing a thing about it. Why was that?"

"Because I knew what was about to come out of her mouth before you did."

"Let's not talk about it now," I said. "Are we going in the same direction as the plesiosaurs? I would love to see them again before we head home."

Bowen looked over at David, and they both shook their heads and rolled their eyes. Maybe they thought I was in denial and I would change my mind? Well, I was not, and I wouldn't be.

***

Captain Harry shut the engines off after thirty minutes, and the anchor was dropped. As we were making our way to our cabins and some others went back to the canteen, Rory jogged up to me and told me the captain wanted a word. He looked devastated. When I asked him if he was okay, he shook his head.

"Yeah, we'll come now," Bowen said. He also looked concerned for Rory and put his hand on his shoulder.

Rory looked around awkwardly before he said, "Harry wanted to speak to the Watcher alone."

I could see from Bowen's face that he was uncomfortable about this. What could Harry possibly want with me? He probably wanted to try to convince me to destroy my Kraken too. I had a feeling I wouldn't be able to shut the discussion down with him as easily as I could with David and Bowen. The last thing I needed right now was to get into a debate.

"I'll be all right," I murmured to Bowen. I turned to face Rory. "I'm ready."

Bowen stayed put while Rory and I walked down the passageway. My heart beat faster the closer we got to the bridge. As far as I was concerned, although written and created in a rage, the Kraken was a blessing. Maybe I could convince him to see it my way?

Rory opened the door, ushered me through and then he left, closing the door behind himself.

Captain Harry was leaning over the control panels with his head hung low. He didn't look up or acknowledge my presence. "Watcher, do you expect me to be grateful and say thank you for my existence and resurrection?" he sighed.

"No." I had never expected that. "I didn't do what I did for a gold star sticker."

"Maybe I should. I am, by the way, grateful for my existence. I wasn't at first, I'll be honest with you. It was confusing at first, when I discovered I had no family or past, and that I was created from your mind, for that matter. You would expect someone like me not to know any different, but I do." He still hadn't turned to face me.

"But you do have a family, Harry. You don't need blood relatives. I certainly don't; I have chosen my family, as you have." And if that wasn't enough, Captain Harry had scored legions of supporters and fans. He'd created an online profile, filming and documenting the *AmberIvy*'s successes, as well as their trials and tribulations. His crew adored and respected him, as did many other seafarers around the world. Unfortunately, that included the poachers, hence having such a large bounty on his head and this ship. But there wasn't one protection vessel that wouldn't come to his aid.

"I know that now. Watching Lana and Rory's relationship blossom has given me hope, as has Tilikum's birth." His head was still hanging low while he said that. His body language was not matching his statements, which confused me.

"Why did you call me here?"

He finally stood straight and faced me, but his sorrowful expression made me nervous. His eyes were wet with unshed tears. "While we were on the move, we received a distress call from the *Ocean Warriors*. A military ship lined up and fired four missiles into their hull—"

"We need to go back. We need to pull up the survivors. Now."

"They're gone. We can no longer detect them on our radar."

Bile rose, my skin prickled, and it felt like my blood had drained from my face to my feet. Harry rushed to my side, grabbing a tin bucket en route, which he handed to me so I could empty my stomach into it.

Harry held my hair away from my face and carried on speaking. "We don't have much time. That ship is heading straight towards us, and I have no doubt that they plan to do the same to us. If you have any control over the Kraken, now would be a good time to say so."

"I don't." I spat the taste of sick out of my mouth. "My telekinesis is stronger than I first thought. If it wraps its tentacles around our ship, I may be able to pry them off gently. That's it."

He was expressionless at first, but then I saw a fire burning in his eyes. They mirrored mine in more ways than one. We were coming to the same conclusion.

"We can't sit here and do nothing," he said to himself.

That once foreign emotion I had developed a while back, buried deep within my bones, now boiled throughout my body. It was pure hatred, and it gave me strength and the clarity I needed. "We need to fight back."

He smiled at this. "It's a risk, but if we stay dead in the water or sail back slowly, they'll catch us up. We'd be at a greater risk."

I nodded in agreement.

He stood and sounded the alarm. Rory and the other two mates came through the door instantly.

"*All souls to the top deck. Weapons at the ready,*" Captain Harry bellowed over the emergency alarm.

Two of them dipped their heads in acknowledgement,

and Rory ran to the control panel. "Captain, there are now three ships heading our way."

"There are?" He looked over his shoulder to see for himself. "Shit. Start the engines. Watcher, tell Bowen to start lowering the small boats. *Go!*"

As I ran through the door, Harry grabbed my arm and stared intently into my eyes; we were almost nose to nose. "The Kraken will come. If it perishes, bring it back. Keep bringing it back. Do you hear me? It's the only chance we have at protecting the plesiosaurs."

I was too shocked to answer.

He shoved a pen and pad in my hands, "I heard you say it in the canteen. You were right. And bring us all back too – I'm not ready to die."

***

I bounced straight off of Bowen's chest when I turned the corner. "Lower the small boats. We have three ships headed our way. They took down …" *Oh no. How do I tell him Nate is gone?* I couldn't.

"Shit. Come on." He grabbed me by the scruff of my jumper and pulled me through the passageway. He stopped to pull two life jackets off the hooks. Three crew members were behind us. He pulled a few more off for them and ordered them to get to their designated boats.

This time, when Captain Harry fired up the engines, it shook the *AmberIvy* to life.

"Hurry, come on," Bowen said.

"We need to find David and Varik."

"*We're here,*" Varik shouted from outside the hatch. He had a smile on his face.

I was about to ask why when I noticed the sun was going

down. He was the greatest weapon we had aboard this ship, and I knew he would be looking forward to the bloodshed.

Bowen started to lift and lower boat one over the deck, using a crane. "Zoe, get in this one and wait for me."

"I need to be up there." I pointed to the crow's nest, "I need to keep an eye out for the Kraken."

"I don't fucking think so." He laughed without humour.

"Bowen, I have a much better chance of protecting this ship with me on it."

"Get in the small boat now, and I'll take you to port. You can protect the *AmberIvy* from there." He pushed me towards the boat.

"It was by chance I was able to bring you back. I will need to know where everyone is at all times so I can write them back into existence." I looked into his eyes. I needed him to understand that I wouldn't be leaving. His eyes watered in frustration. "Please, Bowen, I don't want to go through that again. Plus, this is my fight too."

Lana rushed past us, interrupting what Bowen was about to say. She was holding on to Varik's arm. "We're taking this one. Our vampire wants to eat out tonight."

"I will take out one of the ships," Varik said in our direction. "Bowen, listen to the Watcher. She needs to stay on this ship. You'll see." Both he and Lana got into the boat that was meant for me.

"Lana, does Rory know what you're planning?" Bowen asked, while he lowered the small boat.

"It was his idea," she replied, as she clipped her harness to either side of the steering wheel.

Bowen didn't say anything else. His pained expression had quickly replaced my adrenaline with guilt. We both looked over the railing. As soon as the small boat touched the waves, they were off. Varik put his arms in the air like he was on a bloody roller coaster, and the crew cheered them on. I suppose they didn't need to fear death as they should, which got me thinking.

"Bowen, if we do go down – again – will you still not want me to bring you back?" I held on to him, silently begging him to change his mind.

He sighed before he answered, "David told me what you went through when … The thought of you being in that pain makes me …" He tutted. "Yes, bring me back. But there isn't much you can do if you die, is there? I don't think you or these lunatics have even thought that through."

Was he right? Was I taking too much of a risk by staying on this ship? I felt like I wasn't. I felt like I was exactly where I needed to be. "I'll help you get the boats ready, then I'll climb up to the crow's nest. The sun is almost down. Will you switch on the floodlights?"

"Yeah. Come on then."

***

The flood lights were on, and I could see the deck below clearly, but I couldn't see much further past the hull. It felt like being at home with the lights on when it was dark outside. The moon was full, and I knew it would give me more of an even coverage.

I radioed the bridge and told them to switch off the lights. They didn't question it. As soon as the light died, I saw a ship in the distance.

At first, I thought my eyes were betraying me. I could see movement on their deck, then numerous flares fired into the air. The crow's nest shook, making me jump. It was Bowen climbing the ladder.

"Varik has that ship under control. We're going to sail

straight past it. Are you okay up here? Did you want the lights back on?"

"No, I can see more without them, and I can see movement on their deck. Look."

He looked over and smirked. "They're abandoning ship. They will either head back to their fleet or try to board ours. Captain Harry wants us to sink their boats if they try it."

"Good." And I meant it.

We more distinctly heard screams whistle through the air the closer we got to the ship. The chaos I witnessed seemed surreal; it felt like a hallucination. Varik had clearly shut down the engines and must have dropped anchor. As we came face to face with the ship, we saw blood splattered on the inside of the bridge windows. That ship's crew started to wave their arms in the air to get our attention, and some were desperately trying to lower their boats.

"Bowen, why can't they lower the boats?"

"They look disorganised to me. A lot of them are. Look over there, at the second one in – their small boats are double-stacked to save space. They can't even get the top one off."

It was half off and hanging over the edge. While a crew member was trying to cut the ropes, another one was trying to push the bottom one off and over the railing.

Their terror should have brought a pang to my chest, but it didn't. I have no doubt they would have cheered and laughed when they took down the *Ocean Warriors*. The difference between us and them was that when we took them down – and they were going down – it would be met with our silence.

As we sailed past, side to side with their ship, explosions erupted from underneath their ship's deck. The crew had no choice but to jump into the water.

"Is that Lana?" I saw a single boat in the water and hoped it wasn't one of theirs from the other side of the ship.

He leaned forwards, crushing me into the railing. "Yeah, that's her. She's waiting for Varik."

"What if they try to board her boat?"

"She'll just run them down," he said coldly. Varik had told me that Bowen had been brutal when he had to be. Although, this time, I felt that his coldness came from a place of pain. That feeling was confirmed when I heard him whisper, "For you, Nate."

Tears streamed down my face. To Bowen, he was Nate, but to me, he was still Officer Blake who showed compassion to an abused dog I'd tried to save, what seemed to me like a lifetime ago. He didn't see – as many would have – a savage dog responding to a dog-attack call; he saw what I saw: a frightened animal.

"I can bring the *Ocean Warriors* back." What I really meant was, *I can bring Nate back.*

"No, I don't think he would want that. They're gone."

As we sailed past the sinking ship, we could see the faint outlines of the other two. At this rate, we would be sailing in between them. We would be surrounded. Surely Captain Harry could see that?

"What now?"

Bowen moved me to my left, then he pointed below. "Rory and Oscar are going to take the front boat out. Can you see that chunky rope they're attaching to the back of it?"

I nodded.

"It has metal cords intertwined in it. He will take that small boat with *that* trailing behind him near their propellers, then it will be sucked in and wrap itself around them, bringing the ship to an abrupt stop."

"And it works?" I felt a little doubtful.

"Two times out of ten. Rory will keep trying until he gets it done, then Oscar will detach the cord so they can get away."

I watched them both board the boat as if they were taking a fishing trip. This gave me confidence. I felt more certain now that we could defeat the remaining ships and start our slow journey back. That was if the Kraken didn't make an appearance.

I looked at Bowen. "How will you stop the other ship?"

"You recreated this ship with missiles, so I heard. We will go after the other ship and see how they like it when the shoe is on the other foot."

"Okay, you go back down, and I'll keep a lookout."

He pulled my face to his and kissed me before he climbed down. When I saw him run to the front of the ship, past the bridge, I took the pen and pad that was tucked in my jeans and started writing. My penmanship was diabolical. It had nothing to do with the fact that the *AmberIvy* was swaying. It was because, these days, the only time I wrote by hand was on my hand.

Still, I had to try something …

The AmberIvy *and crew were both blessed and cursed with immortality. They were never to know death or …*

Or what? I didn't know what to write, and I had to keep a lookout. I started to panic when I realised I was writing about the wrong thing.

The poachers facing the AmberIvy *trembled. They had heard many tales about the* AmberIvy. *Some say it can't be sunk, others call it a ghostship …*

Our crew clapped at something I couldn't see.

"What is it?" I called down.

"Rory's stalled that ship over to the right," a crew member shouted.

It was then that I noticed our ship steering to the left. I didn't have long …

The crew were unprepared for this, with many of them never having been on the ocean before. The plesiosaurs were worth millions, and they had been offered a percentage. The promise of hard cash and an early retirement was too good to pass up …

I looked up and noticed we were changing direction again. Why? Bowen was running towards me, taking two steps at a time up the ladder.

"What's going on?" I asked him.

"Rory swung around the other ship to report back. They have Tilikum strapped to the side. We can't touch them. Captain Harry won't allow it."

"What can I do?" I squeezed the notepad in my hand and felt useless. *How can I change the outcome?*

"Zoe, listen. Lana and Varik are on their way back. David and I are going to take two small boats to that ship and see if we can cut Tilikum loose."

"No, you can't do that. You can't take three small boats to a ship that size."

"We have before—"

A thunderous roar erupted from the sea as wave upon mountainous wave of water rose up. The watery mass towered above us, centred between our three ships. Then, as if it had never been there, the sea became flat once more.

Our engines were shut down immediately. The silence that followed seemed to stop time. The other two ships started to fire flares into the air. As they arched over the sky, an idea came to me – one I hoped didn't cost Tilikum her life ...

The Kraken retreated under the waves, only to be threatened once again by the bright lights in the sky. It had no choice but to defend its territory ...

Bowen asked me what I was doing. I answered him and wrote at the same time. "I'm trying to give the Kraken a reason to go after those ships."

A hum from one of the small boats zoomed past us, breaking my concentration. I looked at Bowen for answers.

"Rory and Oscar will be going back to port. It's protocol; if a small boat is in the water when the Kraken makes an appearance, they aren't able to board. It would attract too much attention."

Of course. That had been mentioned in the meeting I wasn't concentrating on. I nodded and carried on writing just as more flares were fired into the air ...

The Kraken had learned not to come up beside one of these strange, metal sea creatures. It swam silently underneath the metal belly and lifted its tentacles up and over the aggressor ...

The sound of crashing waves broke my concentration. I looked over at the ship Rory had sabotaged. The Kraken was doing exactly what I imagined it would do: what I just wrote by hand. The ship screamed in protest as its metal body warped under the Kraken's strength. Two tentacles either side of the ship were tightened as the other four came up to reinforce its grip. The ship was being broken in two.

I radioed the bridge. "Get our engines started." We needed to go straightaway. I may have won this small victory, but I had no idea how long it would take before the Kraken turned its attention to us. I just hoped that Captain Harry would listen.

"Zoe?" he asked.

"*We need to go. Come on, while the Kraken is busy,*" I shouted while I climbed down the ladder.

I looked up and saw Bowen was still at the top. He was mesmerised by what he saw. I hauled myself back up the ladder and shook his life jacket until I got his attention. He glanced briefly in my direction, then back at the Kraken.

"Bowen, we need to go. Come on."

The engine once again vibrated throughout the *AmberIvy*. This must have pulled Bowen out of his trance, as he finally started to climb down. I looked over at the other ship; it was still afloat – barely. We still had time. Bowen gripped the back of my life jacket as we ran to the bridge.

"Take the wheel, Bowen," Captain Harry ordered, as soon as we entered. "Turn her around."

David was on the radio. He wanted confirmation from Lana and Rory, the small boat pilots, that they were still headed back to port in Oban. They may not be in the same boat, but knowing they would soon be reunited went a long way to calming my nerves. He then radioed Penny and told her to be on the lookout for them.

"David, what can I do?" I sounded panicked.

"Poppet, that ship was dead in the water; why do you think the Kraken targeted it?"

"Flares." I pulled my notepad from the waistband of my jeans and showed him.

He frowned. "Flares?"

Captain Harry gave me a knowing look. "Go back to the main deck. Throw every box containing a flare gun overboard. Tell everyone you see on your way not to use them."

"I'm on it." As I ran past them both, I caught a pained expression on Bowen's face. He didn't want us to be apart and neither did I. "I'll be back."

***

When the last flare gun box was gone, I looked back at the carnage we had left behind. I saw nothing in the darkness. If it were not for the chorus of screams, you'd think we were alone out here. The stricken ship shot two more flares into the sky, betraying its location. I highly doubted the other ship from their fleet would be coming to their rescue. At some point, they must have realised that too. There's no honour among thieves, as they say. That being said, we were not as far from them as I thought, which meant the other ship must still be close by.

Bowen grabbed my sleeve as I walked through the bridge door and pulled me to him. I heard David tell Captain Harry that the other ship was coming up beside us.

"Tilikum is still strapped to the side of that ship. David, Bowen, lower two small boats; you" – Captain Harry pointed to David – "take a team of four to free her then head back to port; and you" – he pointed to Bowen – "take the Watcher back."

Bowen nodded in agreement and started pulling me towards the door.

"There'll only be five crew members left if we do," I protested.

"This ship only needs four. Go on."

I looked back at Captain Harry. He took three long strides towards me. "Remember what I told you?"

"Yes."

"Do you still have the notepad? Where is it?"

I tapped my stomach to indicate that it was tucked back under my jeans before I left the bridge. It was time to go home.

CHAPTER 11

B owen put his arm under my knees and lifted me into the boat. I looked over to see David barking orders at his small crew of volunteers.

"What if the poachers start shooting at them while they try to free her?" I questioned.

"It's the risk we all take. Hopefully, they will be too distracted," he said while he was trying to strap me in. His hands were shaking. I picked up the buckle to strap myself in, but he swatted my hand out the way.

"Bowen, I've got this. Lower the boat." My heart bled for him. If it were not for me being here, I knew he would have been calmer.

"Okay, let's go." He nodded to another crew member for them to start lowering the boat from the top.

The *AmberIvy* was going too fast to lower the boats safely. When we hit the water below, a wave smashed us back into the side of the ship. Just like that, I was reminded of my journey here with Varik. I kept my hand on the buckle in case we capsized.

"*Are you okay?*" Bowen shouted without looking back.

"Yeah."

We finally cleared the ship and zoomed past the hull. David's small boat was coming from the other side. They came past us, heading towards the poachers. I made a mental note of all the crew and where they were. If things didn't go to plan, I needed to know where everyone was to be able to write an accurate story.

Bowen looked back, then he slowed the engine. The *AmberIvy* was out of sight. He looked down and punched in the coordinates for our destination.

We were zigzagging from left to right while travelling at full speed. When I remembered the shipwreck debris that littered the surface, I wanted to tell Bowen to stop. His floodlight wasn't that powerful, and he had to make snap judgements at the last second. I didn't have the energy to lift my head when I threw up.

The small boat's radio came to life. Bowen spoke into it. The waves and the wind prevented me from hearing what was being said clearly.

"*Bowen,*" I shouted. "*What did they say?*"

He didn't look over his shoulder when he shouted back, "*Tilikum is free. Kraken is back. AmberIvy is anchored. Ship is following David.*"

The ship must have given up its pursuit, and now the captain wanted to dock. There wasn't anything they could do once we were all on land. When the morning came, both our crews could walk past each other down Oban's high street and not know who one another were. We didn't even know what nationality we had been fighting against, and I very much doubted they knew ours. Their ships could be registered with Russia but owned by China. The crew themselves probably didn't even know who their

164

employers were. No wonder they could never be tracked and seized.

"How much longer?" I queried.

"An hour, maybe less."

From the darkness, a hollow ship's horn could be heard. I wasn't sure which direction it had come from, yet I subconsciously looked back. Bowen's radio crackled. This time I could hear David's voice, but not what he said. Our boat slowed and then stopped.

"We're going to let the ship pass," he said, then he killed the lights.

"Why?"

"The Kraken has attached itself to it. We can't lead it back to Oban."

We were probably too late for that, being this close; still, we had to do what we could.

This time when David spoke, I heard. He was taking the four crew members back to the *AmberIvy*, not only for their safety, but also in the hope of leading the other ship away from land. He told Bowen he would wait by the radio and wanted us to contact him when we made it to land, so he could join us.

This time, the ship's horn was accompanied by flares. They, too, were a lot closer than I thought.

Bowen unstrapped one side of his harness, turned to me, then kneeled right in my sick. The moon provided me with just enough light to make out his features. He looked down, screwed his nose up, then smiled at me. "Are you okay, sweetheart?"

"Yeah, I am. The crew, are they all safe?"

"They're safe." He brushed my hair from my face.

"I think that ship's heading straight into Oban anyway."

"Not if the Kraken takes it down first."

***

The gunfire got louder the closer the ship got to us. It was so frantic aboard their ship that I didn't know where to look first. As they passed, I saw two of their crew members jump overboard. Three of their lifeboats were hanging off the ship. We watched as they turned their harpoon and fired it straight into the bridge. They must have thought they'd have a clear shot towards the back of the ship, which the Kraken was now tightly clinging to. Four tentacles trailed behind the ship. I couldn't help but worry about it getting hurt by the propellers.

Bowen waited until they were clear before he started the engine. This time, we were going a lot slower. The ship and the Kraken faded into the darkness, with only the occasional flare betraying their location.

My heart was lifted when I finally saw the lights from Oban town, but only for a brief moment. The lights also highlighted the outline of the ship in front of us. It didn't seem to be slowing down.

"Bowen, that ship's heading straight towards the ferry port."

He didn't answer. He didn't need to. The deafening screech of twisting metal came through the air. I covered my ears to protect them from the piercing sound. The captain had sailed the ship and crashed it right through the centre of the docked ferry. The ferry now lay on its side, with its underbelly in full view, and was leaning over what had been the loading bay. The poachers' ship's bow was no longer visible.

Bowen aimed for the beach front that was surrounded by the wall I had sat on only days ago. The tide was up. He skimmed around the perimeter of the wall until we found the stone steps. He turned to unbuckle me, but I was already up and ready to get off this boat. I climbed the steps with him right behind me, not even taking the time to secure the boat.

A man at the top grabbed my arm and pulled me up the rest of the way. "Are you from that ship? Do you need medical assistance?" He looked from me to Bowen.

Another roar of twisting metal was carried by the wind. We all looked over at the dreamlike scene.

At first, it looked like the ship was reversing. The Kraken released its hold, one tentacle at a time, only to regrip further up the ship. It was pulling it back into the sea. Small explosions rippled across the ferry as the ship was ripped from it, illuminating the Kraken. It wasn't until people started screaming that I realised the streets were packed.

There was one last explosion before the ship went down. This time, it did not illuminate the Kraken, for it was already under the water. The sea was calm once more, as if what we had seen was nothing but a hallucination. If not for the ferry still being on its side, sirens, and people running back and forth, it most certainly would have felt like one.

"Sweetheart, come here." Bowen stepped in front of me and held me tightly.

I wrapped my arms around him. "We did it."

We both looked up as three helicopters flew over. Their bright lights shone over the wreckage. One landed in the ferry port car park while the other two, I assumed, searched for my Kraken. I looked back at the ferry. I didn't care for the poachers, but the ferry could have had innocent souls aboard. I pushed Bowen out of the way and retched; nothing came up.

"Sit, sit." He rubbed my back. "That's it; it's over now."

One minute, I was on the floor, and the next, I was being lifted, squeezed and then shaken. "Bowen, stop."

"Varik, put her down."

He dropped me on the floor. Bowen pushed Varik out of the way and picked me up. Even though pain shot through my knee, I couldn't help but smile. We would all be together again soon. I stood up to face him. He was grinning, with all his deadly teeth on display. I glanced around to make sure no one else witnessed it.

"Don't worry, little Watcher, everyone here is too distracted." He put his arm around my shoulders and whispered, "Your Kraken was magnificent."

"Varik," Bowen said. "I need to radio the *AmberIvy*. Stay with her."

Varik clapped him on the back before he climbed back down the stone steps. I followed him to the edge, not wanting to let him out of my sight. The small boat had drifted and he had to swim to it. I watched as he was able to lift himself into it with ease.

I heard Captain Harry's voice come through on the radio, but right next to me. "You have a radio?" I frowned.

Varik smirked while he pulled it from his back pocket. He told Harry we were safe, then switched it off. "Why didn't you just give him your radio instead of letting him go back down there?"

"Keep your eyes on Bowen. Gary is behind us."

Bowen was still talking on the radio to the *AmberIvy*. Images flashed through my mind of Ivy's hands wrapped around his head, with her threatening to snap his neck, while his leg was broken. Gary was unpredictable. If he thought to hurt me by hurting Bowen, he would die. I looked around at the crowds of people. There were too many witnesses. I was starting to feel breathless. "What do we do?"

"When the time comes, use your telekinesis to throw him

through the air, then I will deal with him." He stood calmly beside me as if he were waiting for a bus.

"Varik, you can't kill him in front of all these people," I wheezed. Why was I struggling to breathe?

He frowned at me, but he didn't answer.

We needed help. "Where's Rory, Oscar and Lana?"

"Here with Penny."

I looked around for them, while trying to suck in a breath of air.

"Eyes forwards. They should be behind Gary, but with all the commotion just now, I can't be certain."

"What do you think he's planning?" I tried to say. I could feel myself starting to panic. *Just breathe,* I thought. I concentrated on Bowen; he was putting the radio back and was getting ready to jump back into the water.

"He has a machete." He drew in a deep breath through his nose. "I can scent Penny now; she's right behind him."

Bowen started to swim back. I wanted to shout at him to stay back, but I couldn't talk. When my vision started to close in on itself, I fell to my knees.

"Up, little Watcher." He yanked me up, holding me to his side, then he quietly said, "Three, two, one."

"Face me, leech." I heard.

We both turned. Through my hazy vision, I saw Gary's machete raised high in the air, ready for him to swing it down on Varik. I let power run from my core to my hands, wanting to keep Gary's arm in place, but I was too late. It just happened too fast. Varik fell back into my arms. His throat was slashed wide open.

"*No! Varik!*"

When he tried to talk, blood bubbled from his lips instead. Bowen ran to us, then at Gary. Gary slashed wildly at Bowen, never making contact. I allowed power to vibrate throughout my body again. I concentrated on Gary's skull, wanting to crush it. I lifted my hand at the same time Penny smashed Gary over the head with a hammer. His body folded at the knees before he fell to the floor, face first. People started screaming again, reminding me of the crowds we were in the centre of. Right now, they were the least of my concerns.

"*Bowen,*" I screamed. "*Varik isn't moving. He can't die like this. He needs blood. Do something.*"

"I know what to do." He pulled a small knife from his pocket and was about to open up his wrist.

"No, you'll die. He'll take too much." I tried to pry the knife from him, intending to open up my own wrist, when I caught sight of Gary. Penny, Lana, Oscar and Rory were now standing around us. "Bring me his body – *now!*"

Penny's eyes opened wide before realisation struck. She ushered the others to help. They started to drag Gary's body towards us.

"*Hurry,*" I shouted.

David and Goodboy appeared to the side of us. "Bloody hell," he said as he kneeled beside Varik and wrapped his hands around his neck. "Come on, son. Hang in there. Is he gone?"

"*I don't know,*" I screamed.

Gary's body was dumped next to Varik. Penny passed me his wrist; I grabbed it and put it over Varik's mouth. Nothing. I rubbed Gary's wrist on his teeth. Nothing. "Why won't he drink?"

"Here." Bowen slashed Gary's wrist open and let the blood pour into Varik's mouth.

Gary moaned.

"Hurry, Bowen, the emergency services are heading our way," David pleaded.

"I'll distract them. Come on, guys," Penny said as she motioned for the other three to come with her.

"Penny, we need cover. Handle it alone."

She nodded to David while the other three closed in around us. Rory had tears streaming down his face, and Lana looked in shock.

"Please, Varik, please don't die like this." *I know I can bring him back if I want to, but how? Like David and Goodboy. Okay, okay.* My heart rate started to come down when I realised this was not the end. I would find a way. I would always find a way for my family.

Gary once asked me if what I was doing was right. He said that people lose loved ones all the time, and he was right. But if I hadn't been able to do what I can, I would have lost my whole family by now, never to be seen again – including Missy. It didn't matter to me whether it was right or wrong: I couldn't live without them. They were my life; the very air that I breathed.

Varik's eyes flew open, then he clamped his jaws around Gary's wrist. We watched in awe as his neck started to knit back together. He was healing faster with every gulp he took.

As relief swept through me, I watched Gary's eyes flutter open. He was dying. I would take responsibility for his death deep into my soul, and I would one day die with the memory of him still attached to it. I reached over Varik and picked up Gary's other hand. I squeezed it and whispered in his ear, "This is my doing. I'm so sorry."

He squeezed my hand back before it went limp.

It's then I realised that my abilities came with a much steeper price than I had anticipated. Bowen had been right all along. This was what he was trying to protect me from, but I was too arrogant to heed his warning, thinking that I had everything under control after what happened with Amber.

Hearing footsteps pounding the pavement snapped me from my thoughts.

"Hurry; get him up," David said. "Bowen, help me push him and Gary over the wall. I will use your boat and take him back to the *AmberIvy*."

"David?" I wanted to keep us all together, but I knew David was right.

Varik didn't protest when Bowen threw him in the sea. Rory grabbed Gary's shoulders, and David picked up his ankles, and together, they swung him over the wall. Goodboy whined, then jumped in after Varik.

"When will you be back?" I asked.

David kissed me on the top of my head, then said, "Poppet, Varik has a lot of people searching for him. We'll be back in a couple of weeks after everything dies down."

"What about the Kraken?"

"You should have thought about that before you created it," he snapped. Then his features softened before he held me tightly. "We will be okay, don't worry."

I nodded.

He turned towards Bowen. "Tell them we were poachers from that ship."

"Okay, be safe."

David jogged down the stone steps into the water. He pulled Varik's lifeless form to him, then started to swim to the boat.

"Watcher?"

I turned to find Lana, Rory and Oscar standing behind me.

"If you don't need us, we'd like to go back with David and Varik," Rory continued.

"Of course. Thank you ... for everything." I didn't really know what else to say.

"No, Watcher, thank you," Lana said.

Rory picked up Lana's hand and placed a kiss on her knuckles. All three took the steps down and swam to the small boat. Why they wanted to go back to the *AmberIvy* was beyond me. Then I remembered what Bowen had said: some of them lived on that ship. The *AmberIvy* was their home.

Bowen tightened his grip on me while we watched them help David with Varik. Once they were both in, the other three lifted Gary, while David pulled him onto the boat.

"Will they dump Gary's body on the way?" I asked.

"Don't think about that right now. Come on, we need to get out of here."

As we turned, I realised we were too late. The emergency services were running towards us. Penny was with them. She looked all around us for the others, then she stopped.

Oh shit, we're on our own now; not that I blame her. I turned to Bowen. "What do we do now?"

"Say nothing. Let me do all the talking."

"Okay." I wrapped my arms around his waist and pleaded for us not to be separated again.

A police officer looked over at the sound of David starting the engine. I looked back and watched them disappear into the night. When I faced the police officers and emergency crew, I was stunned. Relief swept through me with such force that I could have fallen to the ground.

I saw Penny slowly walking towards us. "You should have seen your face, Watcher."

"That was close," Bowen said, as he watched them run straight past us.

"Actually, it wasn't," Penny said. "I tried to tell them that I found the guy who snatched me. I told them I smashed him over the head with a hammer as well. They couldn't care less. Kraken trumps kidnapping. Where's Varik?"

"David took him back to the *AmberIvy*." I hugged her close and apologised for what she'd gone through.

She shrugged it off. "I'm okay now; don't worry about me."

"What do we do now?" I looked up at Bowen.

He was about to answer when another explosion came from the ferry port. Did anyone get hurt? I hoped not. I could have argued with myself and said this wasn't my fault. I could have blamed the poachers, for killing my plesiosaurs, and Bowen, for forcing me to retaliate the way that I had. It would have been so much easier to blame them instead of myself, but I couldn't. If I had waited, just one more day, then this would not have happened. On the flip side, my plesiosaurs would be safe now. My emotions were once again at war with each other; that was nothing new.

"Come to my dad's for now," Penny said. "If he's in, you can explain to him what happened to his boat, then tomorrow, one of you can scrub all that blood off my driveway."

CHAPTER 12

It had been three weeks since the Kraken was last sighted, and that was in Oban. It was fair to say that my plesiosaurs no longer dominated the news. There were many ships that were unaccounted for, so I knew the Kraken was still out there. And as far as I knew, there were no find-and-destroy missions hanging over its head. I only hoped it could live out the rest of its days in peace.

I was just taking a book that had been sold online off the shelf when I heard the bell go above the shop door; it was Bowen coming back with our lunch.

"I got you your usual." He went to hand it to me, then pulled it back. "Swap it for a kiss."

I smiled before I paid the toll for my baguette. "Was it busy in town?" I asked, before I took a bite. "Ew, falafel."

"Sorry, that's my one." He grinned before swapping them over. "No, the town's dead, as it always is on a Sunday." There was a hint of sarcasm in his voice.

I had woken up this morning not knowing what day it

was. The second my eyes flew open, all I knew was that I had to get back to work. It was time to move on. The police were still looking for Gary, not that they'd ever find him, and their questions came fewer and farther between. Bowen was there with me every step of the way. If he hadn't been, I would have confessed to everything. Still, I was filled with grief, not just for him and my involvement, but for Officer Blake too. What had happened to the *Ocean Warriors* weighed heavily on both our hearts. Bowen's mostly, because he knew first-hand what it felt like to be on a sinking ship with no hope and a zero chance of survival. Bowen now tossed and turned in bed, and knowing that he was suffering tore at my heart. I taught him my breathing exercises, and I told him to get out of bed and read a book whenever he couldn't sleep; I would always get up with him, so that he wasn't alone. I had also asked him about Nate again. I reminded him that not only did Nate know about everything but he accepted it. He would adjust. This time, Bowen said he would think about it. That was enough for me; I wouldn't pressure him.

"Your mum rang while you were out." I told him.

He rolled his eyes.

His mum had been ringing three times a day, every day, since we got back. Not that you could blame her. Penny drove us back to David's car in the morning after we had stayed at her dad's that night. Luckily, my belongings were still in the car, along with the keys Varik had just left in the ignition. We thanked Penny and drove straight to Bowen's mum's home. Fiona screamed when she saw him, kissed him all over his face, screamed again, and then reprimanded him for not calling sooner. After that, she kept frowning at him and giving him double takes, as if she wasn't seeing something clearly. The doubt I saw in her eyes made my heart break. The reason for it was his eyes; he didn't know what to tell her when she asked. He tried to palm her off by saying strange things happened at sea all the time.

She obviously didn't believe him; she just shook her head. "Funny how they are the exact same colour as Zoe's." After that, she said she was just grateful to have him home and told him to leave it at that.

We stayed with her for almost two weeks.

"What did she say?" he asked.

"She asked how we were doing. I told her we were back at work, and she was pleased. She's coming down next week."

We ate our lunch, then we went back to work. We had to refund a few customers because they hadn't received their books while we had been closed. Bowen sent them all an apology and a twenty-percent-off voucher in the hope we wouldn't lose their custom. If I were honest, it was the last thing on my mind.

When it was time to close, I flipped the sign and locked the door. "Do you want a coffee while we wait?"

"Yeah, go on then. I'm sure he will be late anyway."

While the kettle was boiling, I heard a knock on the door. Bowen answered it and cheered because who we were expecting was on time for once.

While they were chatting, I grabbed my comb, scissors and neck trimmers out of my bag, and then wedged them in my back pocket. I hooked the black-and-white striped gown over the crook of my elbow, and I carried out Bowen's and my coffees, with the spray water bottle handle hanging off my little finger.

"Little Watcher." Varik was holding Missy against his chest.

"Hi, where's David and Goodboy?"

"On their way. Goodboy decided to chase after a cat, so David went after him." He put Missy down so she could run around and say hello. She hadn't adjusted as quickly as Goodboy and often ran off. We didn't worry too much, though; she always came home eventually.

"Right." I pulled out a chair from the back. "I'm ready when you are."

I secured the gown around his neck and started spraying Varik's hair to get it wet.

David and Goodboy walked through the closed door. "It's about time he got a decent haircut."

"Not for lack of trying." Varik looked up at me while I was combing his hair.

"Keep your head straight." I tapped the top of his head with my comb. "Have you seen Captain Harry today?"

"No."

"I wasn't asking you. David?"

"Yes, you know I have. They're still docked. The plesiosaurs have moved closer to land now they are safer. Harry says he sees them almost daily now."

I knew what David would say. I had kept in touch with Penny and asked Bowen to contact the *AmberIvy* too – on a daily basis. It lifted my heart to know that all my creations were doing well; they deserved peace. "Did he or anyone else see Tilikum today?"

"No, not today." David smiled. "You know, poppet, I was standing next to him when Bowen phoned … and asked the same question."

"I know, David, but that was earlier today. He could have seen her since."

I would love to travel up there and see them for myself, but I never will – not anytime soon anyway. Scotland had taken the lead in protecting my plesiosaurs. Now, there were fewer ships and my plesiosaurs had moved closer to the coast – sometimes on it – they were able to concentrate their efforts. They'd enforced a new strict border policy, stopping all people from entering their country, both on land and at sea. Only Scottish nationals could leave and re-enter – hence Fiona and Penny having to drive down to see us. Now that a plan of action had come together, the rest of Europe had helped raise funds for the new protection plan. If any ship was found in their territory, without reason, it was blown up, just like that – no questions asked.

The world had changed much since my Kraken had made such a memorable appearance and was caught on camera. Cruise ships were now just being used as docked hotels. All the cheap crap from around the world couldn't be transported, although I was certain it would start coming through the Eurotunnel soon. Fish was also off the menu for the time being, and yet fishing supplies were in demand and at twice the price. I smiled when I remembered reading an article about huge numbers of people taking up fishing. They fished from the coast, rivers and lakes. It always amazed me how new doors opened when others shut, and how quickly people could adapt.

"She's doing well; we'll spot her again soon." He pulled out the stool from underneath the desk and passed it to Bowen while he sat in his chair to resume their game of chess.

I looked over Varik's head at them, then at the dogs. I was content. I had everything I had always wanted, right here, in this shop.

Bowen looked over and mouthed, "I love you," and I mouthed it back.

He knew what I was feeling right now, at this moment. It was pure satisfaction. This was all I wanted from life. My family, my coven and their happiness, and I would do anything in my power to keep it that way.

***

A few hours after we left the shop, I fired up my laptop to reread what I had written before I showed it to Bowen.

"Here." I passed it over to him. "This is her."

He smirked, then pointed to the author name on the screen. "We're not married yet, sweetheart."

"I know. We will be soon, though."

He looked at me as if I were the only woman in the world. "Next month."

I didn't want some flamboyant cupcake wedding with boring speeches and a stupid white dress I would never wear again; I couldn't think of anything worse. So Bowen had agreed to marry me in a registry office.

"Yeah, next month; I can't wait." I smiled. "Read it then, and tell me what you think. I definitely think he's going tonight because he seemed a bit sheepish earlier."

"He did, didn't he?" Bowen looked down at the screen and resumed reading…

The Hellfire Caves
By Zoe Williams

Harper watched as her work colleagues got in their cars to head home. They all waved goodbye as she locked the gate and headed back to the gift shop, where she lived in the back room behind it. Her work colleagues were her family, and they had gone to great lengths to protect her existence. Without them, she would have perished, in more ways than one. She often remembered the time when they had found her. She had been weak and starving.

Harper's parents had left her in the Catacombs

within the Hellfire Caves, before they went to war. Two days had passed when she finally emerged to look for them. She made her way to the River Styx. Without an obol, the gateway looked like any other cave tunnel. Yet, she waited there, every night, until one time when she had collapsed.

Sarah, who is now one of her work colleagues and the manager of the Hellfire Caves, had found her. She had cradled Harper in her arms and had sworn to protect her. Harper thought back to the time when Sarah had taken her home to live with her, but Sarah had soon come to realise that housing a young vampire was near impossible. So, all the staff members who protected the caves and hosted the tours within came together to make sure she could live here as comfortably as possible. And she did. She enjoyed her job in the gift shop and loved her adopted family – and yet something was missing. She was, she had to admit to herself, lonely.

She took out a bag of blood from her fridge and poured it into one of the café's latte mugs. Tonight was warm, so she decided to enjoy her beverage in the walled courtyard garden, just like the tourists had been doing all day.

***

Varik

I would have asked, but I knew he would have said no. So, I just took David's car – again. It wasn't like he had any need for it. I flipped down the mirror to check my hair. The

Watcher had done a good job, even though I told her it was the worst haircut I had ever had. Truth be told, it was the first haircut I have ever had.

A car blared its horn from behind me when I veered off to the centre of the road. Couldn't that fucking idiot see I was looking at my hair? If I had known that picking up my female was going to be this much of a hassle, I wouldn't have bothered.

I picked up my phone off the passenger-side seat to check I was still going in the right direction. I was, and I'd be on the same road for a while yet, which meant I had time to text Bowen.

He replied, "Do not text and drive!"

"Why not?" I texted back, telling him that the Watcher was writing a new story. A story about killer spiders that take over Witney town. I smiled to myself when he rang my phone, over and over. I didn't answer.

As I got closer to my destination, this strange pang hit the centre of my chest. I had experienced it before when the Watcher and I had discussed my female. The Watcher called it nerves. I told her to fuck off, but then I quickly looked it up when she wasn't looking. She was right. I was well acquainted with fear; I had often feared for Goodboy's and my coven's welfare because they couldn't take care of themselves. But I'd never experienced nerves. Nerves were for pussy humans.

The turning to the Hellfire Caves led to a single-track road. A car drove towards me and expected me to reverse. I didn't have time for that shit, so I carried on driving, and lightly tapped his bumper. Finally, the driver got the message and reversed into what looked like a school drive to the right. I shook my head; David was right: some drivers just shouldn't be allowed on the road.

The parking for the Hellfire Caves was steep. I took a moment to look at my previous home; I felt nothing and couldn't be arsed to wonder why. When I got out of the car, it rolled back down the car park. It hit a house, then stopped. At least I would know where it was parked.

"What the hell did you just do?"

Was that a flicker in my heart I just felt? If her appearance was as hypnotic as her voice, then the Watcher had done me proud. I turned. She was standing behind the gates. The light from the moon was reflecting from her dark, waist-length hair. She was exquisite, and she was mine.

Her eyes narrowed. "I said, 'What the hell did you just do?' You're … you're the same as me."

I pointed behind her. "I am the ruler of the Inner Temple."

My female smiled adoringly at me. Of course, she was already infatuated with me. "Liar. Only queens ruled the Inner Temple. What are you doing here?"

"You're my female. I'm here to take you home."

She laughed. "I am home. What's your name?"

She was desperate to know everything about me. I ran my hand through my hair. "I'm Varik, and you are Harper."

"How do you know my name?" She stepped back. She was inviting me in.

I snapped the lock to the gate and walked through.

"Hey, you're going to have to pay for that," she chided.

"I don't have any money," I replied with a grin. "I don't need it."

I looked around the walled garden and took a seat at one of the tables. A black cat jumped down from the wall and curled itself around my female's ankles.

"Go back, Umbra. Shoo, shoo," she said.

It scampered off. I couldn't wait to tell the Watcher where that thing had been hiding.

"Is she yours?" I asked, hoping that it was.

"No. Answer my questions."

So I did. She finally took a seat opposite me and couldn't get enough of me. She asked me a myriad of questions. If I were honest, I rather liked it.

"So, you're the captain of the *AmberIvy*?" she queried.

"I am."

"And you're the Watcher's guardian? And you can teleport?"

"I am, and I can ... soon." I reached over the table to hold her hand, but she pulled it out of reach. Why?

"Is that hurt I see in your eyes, Varik? Who is David again?"

"No, you cannot see hurt in my eyes," I snapped. "I told you, he's my personal assistant."

"Okay ... Well, luckily for you, I don't get out much, and I'm curious about your coven. I would like to meet them." She flicked her hair over her shoulder and pouted.

She was in love with me.

THE END

APPLE TREE

A short story by Kelly Barker

Willow pushed Malcolm's hand away when he reached out to her for the third time. "This is taking longer than I expected," she said to herself. Her brow furrowed. "I'll be back in a moment, darling."

"Will ... ow," he rasped. "Doctor ..."

"My darling husband, you don't need a doctor." She ran the backs of the fingers of her right hand along his jaw. "What you need is in the garden." She stood, put the chair back in the corner of their room, then glanced in the mirror so she could see herself to straighten her long, black dress. Her hand was on the door handle when she remembered something. "Oh, I almost forgot." She walked over to the bed where her husband lay and picked up the bowl from the side table. "I know how important it is to you that everything be put back in its place after it's been used. I'll bring you more soup."

"No … doctor."

"I won't be long." She opened the bedroom door and walked down the stairs to the kitchen. The kitchen was spotless; not at all what it was like when her great grandma was alive. The corner of Willow's lip curled when she pictured how the kitchen once was: herbs hanging from the rack above the window, flour all over the worktop and floor, a pantry filled with jars of jam and beetroot, an apple pie cooling on a chopping board, and there was always something bubbling away on the stove. If she concentrated, she could still smell the aromas from the past. Her half smile faded. "I miss you, Grandma."

Today, of all days, she needed to feel her grandma's presence, and now there was only one place left where she truly felt it: the apple tree in the garden. She put the bowl on the worktop with no intention of washing it up, took a basket from the cupboard, then made her way to the back door. The day was glorious for late October; it could quite easily have been mistaken for spring if not for the few leaves scattered in the grass. Before she made her way to the tree, she looked over to the left at her vegetable patch, making a note of what she needed to relieve her husband's pain, which was planted in between the carrots and brussels sprouts.

The apple tree she sought was magnificent: not only did it tower above the others but it also possessed the strength to hold on to all its leaves throughout winter. She could almost hear her grandma's laughter as she approached it. They had spent so much time under it, come wind, rain or shine. She picked up a couple of fallen apples off the roots that protruded from the ground, then she took a seat upon one, next to the tiny mushrooms that sprung from the damp bark. "Oh, Grandma, I tried to follow your recipe, but he is still struggling to breathe. It's been three days now." She threw one of the apples into the gooseberry bush.

When her grandma died, she had left Willow the house in her will. It was a Victorian house, with bay windows at the front, an outside toilet and no central heating; not that they needed it, because the fire kept the house warm at night and the thousands of books that lined the walls retained the warmth throughout the day. She sighed. If Malcolm hadn't thrown her grandma's books away, she'd know how to help him. Against her will, her thoughts returned to that day.

"This house needs modernising," he had said, shortly after their wedding.

He had stripped the house back to the bricks and mortar. Her grandma's house was now painted grey and white. Her wicker chairs had been replaced with a grey corner sofa, and her oak dining room table had been replaced with a glass one. Willow had only agreed to the renovation because Malcolm had promised her he would build her a new bookcase for all her books, but he never did. He had said that the builders had thrown all her books into the skip; therefore, she no longer needed one.

"The books wouldn't have gone with the new interior. Why can't you understand that? Look how much nicer it looks without all that clutter," he had said sharply, while she wept. "You should be grateful I took the time and had the money to make this house liveable."

Willow had regrettably argued that it was actually her money that had paid for this so-called 'higher standard of living'.

She threw another apple into the gooseberry bush. Some of those books had been hand-written by her grandma. They were filled with not only her grandma's recipes but her grandma's mother's and grandmother's recipes too.

The only recipes she could remember now were the ones her grandma had told her under this tree. Her thoughts returned to the time when they were cutting the apples into quarters to scoop out the seeds.

"Now, remember, we need exactly two hundred and one apple seeds," her grandma had said.

"Why two hundred and one, grandma? Why not just two hundred?" the much younger Willow had asked.

"The extra one is for luck, my sweet girl."

"And what are we making?" she queried, while popping three more seeds into the jar.

"We're going to make a special apple pie for your grandad. He has been very angry lately, and this will cheer him up."

She looked up at her grandma's bruised eye. "Why has grandad been angry at you?"

"It's the drink; it makes him do stupid things," was all she had said.

After her grandad had died, the house had become a haven. No more shouting and slamming furniture around, and no more hitting or hair-pulling. She and her grandma had finally found peace; not that Willow had known any different until then. Thank our Mother that her husband was nothing like her grandad. She had been pleased when she learned her husband never drank a single drop. He said he didn't like to feel out of control – something she now more than understood.

Her husband was a doctor. They had met shortly after her grandma had died, when she had fallen into a deep depression. He'd told her she was just grieving and was perhaps lonely. He said that all she needed was someone to talk to. He was right. He had made several house calls to see how she was getting on with the grievance counsellor before he suggested they meet for coffee. She smiled to herself when she remembered the phone call and how he had asked so confidently. No, not asked – suggested. Her heart had instantly been lifted; there was a light at the end of her very dark tunnel. They had fallen in love almost immediately. He had been so impressed with her house when she first invited him over for dinner.

"A house like this must be worth a fortune," he had said.

Three months after their first coffee date, he had taken her to Rome and asked her to marry him. Another three months after that, they were married. Everything had happened so fast that it felt as if the rug had been yanked from beneath her feet. But wasn't that what love was: to feel swept off your feet?

Willow plucked a few of the mushrooms from the apple tree's roots, then she put them into her basket. The mushrooms were called *Amanita phalloides*, also known as deathcap mushrooms. She was proud of herself for remembering what they were called when other memories of her grandma came to mind. Her grandma had been so knowledgeable about plants. She'd spend hours telling Willow what they were called, where they had come from and their numerous uses. She had told her about the legends that accompanied them too: how Norse Berserker warriors had taken *aconite* (wolfsbane) to shapeshift into werewolves before battle, or how witches would rub *belladonna* into their thighs to enable them to fly on their broomsticks. Her grandma had also taught her that everything Mother Nature created had a purpose and how important it was to give back what we took. Willow had never fully understood the meaning of that until she helped her grandma bury her grandad under the bramble bush. The blackberries had been divine and plentiful the following year.

Now, there was one more thing she needed to help her poor husband: hemlock. As she was about to stand, she noticed a black toad resting on her dress. "Hello, little one. It's too cold for you to be out now." She cupped the toad in her hands and placed it in her basket.

On the way back to the house, she stopped at her vegetable patch. The hemlock had wilted, but that mattered very little; it was the roots that she needed. Willow kneeled in the soil, not caring that her dress was now dirty. She used her fingers like a rake to loosen the soil, then she started pulling out of the ground what looked like skinny parsnips. She pulled up as many as she could find this time. *Too many is better than too few,* she thought. Then she carefully lifted the toad from her basket, placed it in the shallow hole, and then covered it with the loose soil and fallen leaves. "You need to sleep, little one. I will see you next year."

***

While Willow was boiling the hemlock roots and mushrooms in a pot, she heard a thump from upstairs. Her dear husband must have fallen out of bed again. "I'm coming, darling," she called out, hoping he'd heard her. Bless him, he was in so much pain, but he wouldn't be for much longer. She quickly added salt and pepper, then poured the soup into the bowl. She didn't bother with a tray as she made her way out of the kitchen to the stairs.

As she rounded the corner, she jumped when she saw her husband's hand clawing over the top step. "Oh, darling." She put the soup down and took two steps at a time to reach him.

He was wheezing and couldn't talk.

"It's okay." She brushed his fringe out of his eyes. "I'm here now."

Not knowing any other way to get him back into the bedroom, she grabbed him by the ankles and dragged him while he was on his stomach. He tried in vain to hold on to the top step, but he was too drained. Once they were inside, she knew it would be impossible to lift him onto the bed, so she grabbed his pillow, put it beside his head, then rolled him over.

"Willow ... please." He tried to reach out to her.

"I'll be right back. My soup will ease your pain, I promise." She rushed out of the room, then came back again with the bowl.

"No, Willow ... please."

She put the soup on the side table and took another pillow off the bed. Her husband flinched when she brought it over his face. She looked from him to the pillow, frowned, then looked back at him. "Don't be silly," she chided with a smile. "I just need to prop your head up a little higher so I can feed you." She gently lifted his head and lowered it onto the pillow.

When Willow kneeled beside her husband with the soup, he tried to push her away. His feeble attempts were spilling the soup from the bowl.

"Malcolm, we can either do this the easy way or the hard way. Don't make me sit on you."

"Why, Willow? Why?"

"Because you wanted to cut my grandma's apple tree down, that's why."

***

One year later.

Willow sat under the tree with one of her new books and her lunch. She had made herself an apple and cinnamon pie. The apples from her tree had been perfection this year; full-flavoured, brightly coloured and bigger than any other year she could remember. She looked over her shoulder at the loose soil between the roots of the tree. Her grandma was right: to fully reap the gifts Mother Nature has given us, you must give back what you take.

THE END

Dedicated to my great grandmother, Isobel O'Leary.
I miss you, Nan.

ACKNOWLEDGEMENTS

I would like to thank Mike, who has supported me from the very start, and Mark Warrick, who corrected my many bloopers (muzzle, not snout) and helped me delve deeper into our own town's myths and legends. I would also like to thank David Hill, who brought the Hellfire Caves map to life, and Troubador publishing for all their hard work and patience. I really hope I have done Witney proud, if not, I will go into hiding.

ABOUT THE AUTHOR

Kelly Barker was born in Oxford and moved to Witney ten years ago for work. She has been a barber since 2002, and loves her job. The protagonist of her debut novel, *The Inner Temple*, is also a barber. She has had many authors in her chair over the years, and has been inspired by them all.

ABOUT THE AUTHOR

This book is printed on paper from sustainable sources managed under the Forest Stewardship Council (FSC) scheme.

It has been printed in the UK to reduce transportation miles and their impact upon the environment.

For every new title that Matador publishes, we plant a tree to offset CO_2, partnering with the More Trees scheme.

For more about how Matador offsets its environmental impact, see www.troubador.co.uk/about/